Patrick's Promise

by

JoMarie DeGioia

PUBLISHED BY:

Bailey Park Publishing

Patrick's Promise

Book Two of the
Braunachs of the Dell Series

by

JoMarie DeGioia

Prologue

Meath Province, Ireland 1810

"MacDonald…"

The voice reached out to Patrick MacDonald, winding itself around him in a teasing caress. He walked through the cool twilight, into the shadowed woods. His stumbling feet seemed to move of their own accord, taking him away from his home. Away from his family. The lure of the voice was too great to ignore.

A laugh came through the mist then, high and soft and promising pleasure. His body reacted and he searched through the trees for the source of the beguiling sound. There, in a shaft of light from the rising moon, stood a beautiful woman. He stared into large eyes the color of the darkening night.

"Who are you?" he asked the vision.

The woman laughed again, throwing her head back as her long golden hair floated around her. Her dress of white clung to her curves, and the sight made his throat go dry. The whisper-thin fabric brushed over shapely legs and touched the tops of her delicate bare feet. With graceful hands, she gestured to him to come closer. He watched, mesmerized by her motions as desire pounded deep in his veins.

"Come to me, MacDonald," she purred.

This is wrong. His mind whispered within, telling him to leave the woman alone. His honor demanded it. He swallowed hard and shook his head. "Nay."

The girl reached out and grabbed his hand. A spark flashed through him, setting him on fire. Under her spell, he stepped closer to her. She kissed him. Caressed him. His body burned as his mind's protests weakened. Deeper into the woods she pulled him, urging him closer and closer.

Patrick glanced down then and saw she floated above the ground, the grass barely touching her toes. A moment of clarity struck him and he pulled away.

"You… you're a Banshee!"

She smiled, and any protest he'd thought to make was lost.

"Aye, Braunach," she purred. "Make me scream…"

Chapter 1
Meath Province, Ireland, 1814

Patrick came awake with a jerk, his body drenched with sweat despite the chill in the room. The nightmare had come again. The memory tortured him with startling regularity as it had the past four years. He rose from the bed and crossed to the washstand, the dark desire slowing ebbing from his body. He splashed his face with cool water from the basin and took a deep breath.

"When will these bloody dreams stop?" he growled.

He settled back on his rumpled sheets and hung his head. Those weeks of insanity four years ago, that time when lust ruled any good sense he had, still preyed on him. Lord, the bitch had left her mark on more than his mind.

He reached up with his right hand and brushed the lines of ridged skin over his left shoulder blade. He tore his hand away and fisted it. The mark still burned on nights like this, a reminder of his sin with the Banshee. He kept the scar hidden from his family and would continue to do so. But it grew harder and harder to live the lie.

He stretched out on the bed once more, his heart finally

slowing its beat. His brother slept on the other side of the wall, his uncle in the wing at the back of the house. They were Meath Braunachs all, and as honorable and true as those who had come before. He had been proud to count himself among that pure tradition. Until the Banshee had bewitched him.

His Uncle Seamus made much use of a magic amber pendant over the years, traveling to many different times and places to bring back tales to delight Patrick and his brothers. Were Patrick to make use of his uncle's amber and leap to the future, his looks would ensure his acceptance among the mortals. And he was handsome enough to draw the notice of the mortal females, though that meant nothing to him now.

Patrick grunted. Escaping to the future wasn't an option for him. He'd committed his sin, and had since sworn himself to celibacy. Never again would passion rule him. He would continue his work in his family's workshop, crafting the finest shoes and boots for those in Meath Province and beyond. He would keep to himself and endeavor to be the man he was before that first fateful walk into the woods: a man his family—and he himself—could be proud of again.

'Twas a pity he had no idea how to accomplish that.

Patrick stood at his workbench the next afternoon, polishing a leather boot until he could see his reflection in its surface. His younger brother, Sean, stood at the other side of the space, hammering tiny nails into the thick sole of a sturdy work boot. Like Sean, Patrick wore breeches and fine MacDonald boots. The men worked in their shirtsleeves, rolled up in deference to their work. Sean hummed a song to himself, but Patrick remained quiet.

Through the open windows came the sounds and smells of spring in the dell, and Patrick breathed in the scents of earth and grass and flowers. Warm sunshine slanted across the room, glowing mutely over the wide plank floor. Yet Patrick felt disconnected. A bird called in the distance and he felt an icy shiver crawl up his spine.

"What ails you, brother?" Sean asked.

"Hmm?" Patrick shook his head to dispel his unease. "It's nothing."

He looked out the nearest window, seeing only sunshine and the fresh colors of the growing earth. There was no sign of the bird that had called. Well, he wouldn't look to the woods. Nay, not after last night's dream. Dark shadows still clung beneath the thick trees there, huddled and hiding among the brush.

"Luke should be back soon," Sean remarked. "Been gone nearly a fortnight."

Luke was their oldest brother who traveled to the future four years ago to reclaim their family's gold and restore their uncle's health. He'd returned with a Pixie for a wife, of all things. Patrick had been stunned to see the girl from the future wrap his brother around her delicate finger. But then again, he had never seen a happier man.

"The wee one likes to travel," Patrick smiled.

Luke's son, Bryce, was just three years old, yet he already possessed both his father's charm and his mother's magic. It seemed like Luke had found more treasure than gold on his journey.

"Keeps him out of the workshop," Sean said.

Patrick managed a laugh at that and the two men returned their attention to their respective tasks. Patrick didn't begrudge Luke's well-deserved fortune, a family Patrick would give his life for if their situations were reversed. But now he was marked to live out his life on the fringes of that happiness. To never know what it was like to love and be loved in the purest sense.

"Master Patrick!" a female voice cried.

Patrick and Sean exchanged a glance of confusion. Patrick looked out the window to see Mrs. O'Grady, the widow who kept their house, hurrying toward the workshop. Her face was red with exertion as she huffed and puffed.

"What the devil?" Patrick murmured.

Sean's eyes grew wide. "You don't think Uncle's ill again!"

"Nay," Patrick said quickly, refusing to consider the possibility. He wiped his hands on a rag and walked to the front of the workshop as Mrs. O'Grady rushed in. "What is it, Mrs. O'Grady?"

"Is it Uncle Seamus?" Sean asked.

The lady shook her head. She mopped her brow with the corner of her apron and straightened the gray curls that had escaped her mop cap.

"Oh! Nay, nay. Seamus be fine." She held out a folded piece of paper toward Patrick. "Master Patrick, this arrived for ya'."

Patrick stifled a shiver as he glanced at the ordinary-looking letter. It was creased and soiled and bore a glob of wax with no seal that he could recognize.

"Who brought it, pray?" he asked Mrs. O'Grady.

She shrugged her round shoulders. "Don't know." She took

11

a breath. "'Twas left outside the front door."

After a brief hesitation, Patrick took the note from her and turned it over in his hands. No address showed on the back, just his name scrawled in a spidery hand.

"What is it, Patrick?" Sean asked.

Patrick shook his head at his brother. He didn't want to guess what the letter might mean. Just touching the filthy thing caused another chill to chase up his spine. But he wouldn't worry his uncle's housekeeper.

He nodded to Mrs. O'Grady. "Thank you, Mrs. O'Grady. I'll take care of this."

The lady nodded in return, relief clear in her brown eyes. "See you lads at dinner, then."

The brothers watched as the lady bustled out of the workshop. When she was good and gone, Sean stepped closer to Patrick.

"You know who it's from," he stated.

Patrick didn't want the letter to have anything to do with last night's dreams. But the odd sensation that had gripped him upon waking wouldn't leave him be. And all Faery folk knew it was foolish to ignore one's intuition.

"I'm not certain," was all Patrick would say to his

brother.

He broke the dirty wax seal and read the contents of the letter. The note was written in a careless hand, brought about by either haste or illness, and urged him to come at once. He recognized it for the summons it was and a tightness settled around his heart. He was called to a village on the other side of the woods. *Damn.*

Patrick stuffed the note into his pocket and grabbed his jacket from a peg near the bench. "I have to go."

He strode toward the door but Sean reached out to grab his arm. "What is it, for God's sake? You're white as down!"

Patrick shook free of his brother's hold. "It's nothing, I'm sure. But I have to go."

Without another word to Sean, Patrick left the workshop and headed for the woods. He'd been called to a cottage he'd never seen in a village he'd only heard of by a person he'd never met.

It was deathly quiet here, and no children's laughter or jingles of horses' harnesses or neighbors shouted greetings could be heard as he left the dell behind him. The smells of decay reached his nostrils, and the air was heavy with the scent of moldy leaves, rotten pine needles and dead wood.

Shadows seemed to cling to his fine boots as he tromped

toward the far village, as if urging him to stay in the dell and leave this dark task to another. There was no one but Patrick for this, however. The letter made that as clear as the water which streamed through the brook behind Uncle Seamus's cottage. And as cold.

Patrick exited the woods after nearly an hour's walk, feeling as though leagues now separated him from home. This village was much like their dell, although shabbier to his eyes. Dirty stoops squatted in front of worn cottages and weeds trailed over the paths leading to their doors. The bright afternoon sun did little to cheer the place as Patrick walked down the center of the dusty street toward his destination. Few inhabitants were out, and those who were showed little joy on their faces. Dingy clothes and unkempt hair were the only impressions he got, since they abruptly turned away from him.

Patrick took the note from his pocket and read the direction to the cottage. He spied the lane up ahead and soon turned down the overgrown path.

The cottage he sought was topped with a sagging roof, and its walls were badly in need of white wash. Weeds choked the flowers attempting to color the place in the meager planting beds flanking the low stoop. There was no way to delay this visit, however. Patrick stepped over the scrub and rapped on the rough-hewn door.

"Come in," a reedy female voice said.

Patrick opened the door and stepped into the dim interior. The room was filthy and smelled stale. Grime from the dirt floor covered his boots after he took but a few steps into the cottage.

He stood in what must serve as a drawing room, though there was little to recommend the place but sagging furniture and threadbare carpet, all of undistinguishable color. Light flickered from a chamber down a short hall and he walked toward it.

"Madam?" he called softly.

Coughing came, along with another summons. "Come here, lad."

Patrick stood in the doorway of a narrow bedchamber and eyed the thin form on the bed. An old woman clothed in a ragged nightgown peered up at him. He couldn't guess her age. Beneath a fringe of tangled white hair, her eyes seemed familiar as she blinked up at him, though.

"Patrick MacDonald?" she asked, her voice weak.

"Aye, Madam." Patrick swallowed and bowed his head. "I am Patrick MacDonald."

She smiled her obvious relief and struggled into a seated position. "Oh, the spirits have a bit o' kindness left for an old woman." She waved a bony hand in the direction of the chair beside her bed. "Sit, MacDonald. Sit. For I have a tale to tell ya'. And a promise to get in return."

Patrick sat, and then his eyes darted about the chamber. A pallet lay on the floor in one corner, covered with what he guessed was once a colorful quilt. He hadn't seen a dog about the house, but no doubt the animal used the nest of blankets in the cool evenings. He looked back at the old woman, at those eyes that were a watery mix of black and purple.

"What is this about, Madam?" he asked.

She coughed again, her body trembling as she sucked in another breath. After she settled back on her pillow she eyed him closely. Her interest was unsettling and his skin tingled.

"Aye, I see him in ya'," she said with a nod. "No doubt ya' will, too."

Patrick blinked. "Who, pray?"

The old woman grabbed his hand and held on with a strength that surprised him. "Yer son."

Patrick stared at her, shaking his head. "Nay."

16

She nodded and squeezed his hand tighter still. "Aye, yer son. My witch of a niece left the babe in my care these past three years."

In the next moment the truth struck Patrick deep to his soul. He yanked his hand from hers. "The Banshee," he rasped.

"Aye." Another bout of coughing came before the old woman continued. "I can't care for the wee one no longer, MacDonald. Take him. Take him back to yer family."

"Nay!" Patrick struggled to his feet, knocking the chair over in his haste. "I won't listen to this madness!"

"'Tis not madness. Well, 'tis madness of a sort." Those eyes, so like the Banshee's, turned toward the doorway. "Ah, here be the wee one."

Patrick turned slowly toward the door, at first seeing nothing but a young woman in dingy clothes. She reached behind her and shoved a little boy into the room.

"Come on with ya'," she sneered.

The child stood still, leaning against the girl's legs. Patrick took halting steps toward him. Though the boy's hair was dirty, Patrick could see his curls were the same reddish brown as his own. Even his eyes were the same shade of blue. Not the Banshee's eyes then, Patrick realized with relief. But the boy

17

wasn't right somehow. He stared through Patrick. His mouth was slack and his skin pale beneath smudges of dirt.

His stomach pulled tight, Patrick whirled on the old lady. "What ails this child?"

She let out a sigh and shook her head. "Surely ya' can guess, MacDonald."

He turned back to the boy. Reaching out, Patrick touched his cheek. The boy let out a short scream and scurried to the pallet on the floor. He began to rock back and forth as strange sounds came from his slack mouth.

"Devlin!" the young woman scolded. "Oh, the lad be the very devil."

With that, she quit the room. Patrick watched as the boy hugged his bony knees to his little chest, blessedly quiet now as he continued to stare at nothing.

Patrick began to turn back to the bed. "Madam, what do you propose I do with him?"

"Take the boy," the old woman whispered. "I can't no more."

She coughed again, a weak sound now in the darkened room. Patrick saw that the child still rocked on his pallet and his heart ached for the little boy. He faced the old woman once more, but she was gone. Just like that, she had breathed her last. The boy had no one now.

Patrick's heart began to pound. He knew nothing of caring for a child, let alone one so disturbed. He could get that girl back, though even as the thought formed he couldn't condemn the boy to the harridan's care. Maybe Luke's Pixie would know what to do with Devlin.

He came slowly toward the pallet and crouched down. "Hello, Devlin," he said softly. He stared down at his fisted hands and forced calm in his demeanor. "I'm your father."

As he spoke the words, an odd ache began in his heart. This child was born out of lust and not love. The boy was cursed in his mind and his soul. And he was his. His. He felt it.

The child said nothing, just continued to stare at a spot on the floor. Though fearing he would scream and pull away once more, Patrick touched Devlin. But the child was like he was made of rags, his muscles were so limp.

Patrick removed his jacket and wrapped it around the boy. He scooped Devlin into his arms. It was as if he weighed nothing at all.

Devlin's body was as still as the old woman's on the bed. If not for the slight rise and fall of his narrow chest, Patrick would think he didn't even breathe.

"Come, son," Patrick said, his throat tight. "We're going home."

He stood and carried Devlin out of the dirty cottage. He was taking his son back to the dell.

Chapter 2

As they neared the dell, night was nearly upon them. The boy hadn't stirred, to Patrick's relief. But, and far more disturbing, he hadn't made a sound either. A stranger comes into the old woman's cottage and takes him away and he has no reaction? His brother Luke's son would have peppered him with questions for the whole of the hour's walk until Patrick was ready to growl. But Devlin? There had been no sound, no sign of recognition or alarm, since Patrick had lifted him from the filthy pallet in the corner.

Patrick had the opportunity to study his son as he walked. The boy had the look of a MacDonald, 'twas true. But Patrick had no doubt that the twisted soul of a Banshee had left its mark on the child. Ah, he dared not think of what he condemned his son to on those long-ago encounters in the woods.

Reared in the dirty little cottage with none but a witch to raise him was another sin, another curse brought about by Patrick's lusts. His weaknesses. His arms tightened around the child and Patrick began to make an apology. When he saw nothing had changed on Devlin's slack features, he closed his mouth.

They came to the house at last, and Patrick nearly shouted

with relief.

"We're home, Devlin," he told his son.

The child gave no indication that he either heard or understood. It was no surprise, that. Patrick placed him on his feet, holding tightly to one shoulder, and stilled before the front door.

He could hear the familiar voices from within, his uncle and Sean discussing something or other and laughing with ease. That would change the instant they knew of Patrick's perfidy. He would be forced to acknowledge his sin and the lies since, too.

He placed his hand on the knob. *Lord, give me strength,* he prayed. Bracing himself for the coming disclosure, he opened the door and stepped inside.

He urged Devlin in before him, and the boy stumbled before standing on shaking legs.

Placing a hand on Devlin's lank curls, Patrick attempted to gather strength. "Uncle."

Talk stopped around the table. All three people in the room turned to face Patrick and his son. Mrs. O'Grady gasped. Sean stared. Uncle Seamus blinked.

Seamus was the first to recover. "'Tis about time,

Patrick. We didn't wait supper for ya'." He placed his napkin beside his plate and stood.

Patrick braced himself for the onslaught of questions, but Seamus simply ran his gaze over the child and asked, "And who be this little lad?"

Devlin leaned against Patrick's leg, but Patrick didn't dare wish it was due to any connection the boy felt. Nay, it was no doubt fatigue that caused him to do so. Nevertheless, Patrick's wish for his own strength turned into a need for his son to feel safe. It was amazing, this connection forged so quickly. More Banshee magic, no doubt.

"This is Devlin," Patrick said.

The knowledge was there in his uncle's green eyes, the conclusion he himself made upon seeing the boy. Seamus looked at Patrick then and gave a curt nod. Relief nearly caused Patrick to collapse against the doorway.

"Mrs. O'Grady," Seamus began, turning to the housekeeper. "Pray see to the boy? He looks like he could use a bath and a change of clothes."

The woman seemed to recover in the next moment. She clicked her tongue and wiped her hands on her apron. "Aye, Master Seamus. And I wager we have some of Bryce's things for the mite to wear."

Patrick's belly clenched. Bryce, Luke's son. He was the same age as Devlin but the two children were as different as could be. Bryce was as bright as the sun while Devlin... Devlin was the moon shrouded in clouds.

Patrick pushed that thought aside. "Thank you, Mrs. O'Grady." He bent down to Devlin. "Devlin, you go with Mrs. O'Grady. She'll see you clean and comfortable."

Again, no response came from his son. No blink, no murmur, no movement.

"There, now," the lady cooed, taking Devlin's limp hand in hers. "We'll have you right and tight in no time, laddie."

Devlin let the woman tug him along, stumbling behind as if he had no control of his little legs. His throat tight, Patrick watched until the pair disappeared down the hall toward his bedchamber.

"Tell us, Patrick," Seamus said.

Patrick turned and sat at the table, burying his face in his hands. The time for lies was over, and relief nearly floored him. "The boy is mine."

"Nay!" Sean gasped.

"Hush, Sean," their uncle said. He sat across from Patrick. "'Tis true, he has the look of a MacDonald."

"But who, Patrick?" Sean asked. "Who is the boy's mother?"

Patrick knew there was nothing else for it. With trembling fingers he unbuttoned his shirt. The scar tingled as if it anticipated its reveal. He pulled down the left shoulder of his shirt and turned away from the table.

"Look at the mark," he said softly. "Surely that will tell you all of it."

No one said a word for a long time. Patrick glanced over his shoulder as his uncle reached toward him. Seamus at last dropped his hand on the table.

"A Banshee, then," he stated.

"A Banshee," Sean repeated in a low, awed voice. "But… the mark be on your shoulder, not your face."

Patrick nodded and pulled the fabric over his scar once more. According to legend, should a man accost a Banshee and force himself on her, she would leave a mark of five fingers on his face. But this was not assault. Time and time again she had called him to sin. And time and again he had indulged her. And himself.

25

"I didn't take advantage of her, Sean," Patrick said. "It's true she bewitched me, but I was willing."

Sean lowered his troubled eyes to his clenched hands resting on the table. Uncle Seamus leaned toward Patrick, his eyes reflecting the pain Patrick felt at the disclosure.

"When did this happen, lad?" Seamus asked.

"Four years ago, Uncle."

"Ah," Seamus sighed. "In the time of my sickness. If I had been in my right mind, she couldn't have taken such advantage."

"Nay, Uncle," Patrick cut in. Now he understood Seamus's expression. "Your mind was gone then, but even if you were whole and sound you couldn't have kept me from going into the woods. From going to her."

His uncle nodded with obvious sorrow.

"Where was the child all this time, brother?"

A flash of recollection struck Patrick of the dark, dirty cottage and the indifferent care by an old witch. "An old crone had him, Sean. The Banshee's aunt."

"He was raised by a Banshee?" Uncle Seamus asked.

Patrick snorted. "Hardly. The boy slept on the floor like a dog."

Seamus straightened to his impressive height and gave a firm nod. "The boy is a MacDonald, Patrick. Your son. From this moment on, we'll see he gets the proper care."

Patrick let out a breath. He took his uncle's hand in his. "I thank you, Uncle. Though the Lord knows I can't reach Devlin."

"He be fey," Sean whispered. He straightened. "Oh! What of Brianna?"

"Aye, Patrick," their uncle said. "Luke's Pixie might be able to reach through to the lad. She possesses strong magic."

Patrick nodded, and hope began to flutter in his chest. Back in that cottage on the other side of the woods he'd wondered about taking Devlin to Brianna. But to have his family bring up the suggestion gave him cautious hope.

"Aye," he said. "I'll ask Brianna to see Devlin on the morrow."

A child's scream came from the back of the house, from the direction of Patrick's bedroom. His heart pounding, Patrick rushed into the chamber to find Devlin huddled in a ball on the floor, his damp curls standing on end. He rocked and mumbled and stared straight ahead. Mrs. O'Grady stood beside the bed, her face as white as the sheet of toweling in her hand.

"He was fine one moment, Master Patrick," she rushed out.

"I washed and dressed him. But when I put him on the bed he… he…"

Patrick held up one hand. "It's all right, Mrs. O'Grady. I'll look after Devlin now."

She nodded and dabbed her eyes with the toweling. "Aye." She walked to where Patrick's uncle and brother stood in the hall. "There be nothing to him, poor mite. I'll make some broth and see if he'll eat."

"Thank you, Mrs. O'Grady," Patrick heard his uncle say. "Patrick?"

Patrick turned and waved a hand at his uncle. "You needn't trouble yourselves this night. I'll see to the boy."

After a moment, the other two men left him to his confounding task. Patrick had no real notion of how to handle the boy, but this was his duty alone. His family willingly gave him their support tonight. He wouldn't ask for more.

Devlin was quiet now, though his slight body still trembled. He looked lost in Bryce's clothes and Patrick's heart clenched again. He placed his hand on Devlin's bony shoulder, earning a flinch he felt to his soul.

"Easy, Devlin," he whispered. "Easy."

He gently lifted the boy and placed him on the bed. When the child didn't fight him in that, he urged him onto his side and drew the clean soft blanket up to tuck beneath his little chin. Devlin shivered and burrowed into the bedding. Like an animal, Patrick thought with anger. Damn the old witch. And damn the bloody Banshee!

"You won't sleep on the floor again, Devlin," he said softly. "You'll have food and warmth and comfort."

And love, he longed to add. But there was no love left in Patrick's wounded soul to give.

He straightened, studying his son as he lowered the lamp in the room. He'd bring in a little bed for the boy in the morning. He would keep this small promise, at least.

***

"Say it isn't so, brother."

Patrick sighed and nodded to his older brother. "Aye, Luke. I have a son."

Luke crossed his arms and leaned against his workbench. "Sean says he's not right."

Patrick laughed without humor and rubbed a hand over his face. "That's putting a shine on it, I daresay. The boy needs help, Luke. Help I can't give him." He stifled a yawn. Lord, he'd gotten little sleep last night, worrying over his son. "Pray, let Brianna come see him?"

"Aye," Luke agreed. "She's gifted with more than one power."

Again, hope began to bloom in Patrick's chest. "I pray you're right, brother. Devlin is…. Ah, it's not his fault he's the way he is."

"It's not yours, either," Luke countered.

Patrick couldn't correct Luke's assertion. He shook his head. How would his brother understand that Patrick's sin was the cause of all of this? That his weakness had led to Devlin and his troubles?

"I have to get back to him," Patrick said. "Pray, tell Brianna we're waiting for her?"

Luke grabbed Patrick's arm as he walked past. "Devlin is a MacDonald, brother. He's family. Our family. You can count on us."

Tears pricked at the back of Patrick's eyes. He swiped at them, and then gave Luke a nod and left the workshop.

As he walked toward the house, more than one person in the dell regarded him with open curiosity. And a wariness he'd never seen before. Their eyes were narrowed as they watched him walk past, their expressions hard.

The blacksmith stepped out of his stall, wiping his smudged hands on the apron stretching across his middle.

"MacDonald!" he called. He was the first to speak to Patrick outside of his family this morning.

"O'Malley," Patrick said in greeting.

A dark look crossed the man's face. "Heard tell ya' have a changeling."

Patrick's back stiffened. He wouldn't spare the man a response. People in the dell knew well of magic, light and dark. Faeries had lived among them for centuries. Surely more than one person saw him carrying Devlin last night, then. And his resemblance to Patrick was no doubt seen in an instant. Well, he wouldn't allow them to slight his son because of his mother's darkness. Or his father's sin. He walked on.

He spied two young women who over the past few years let it be known they'd be open to any arrangement Patrick might propose. He'd never taken advantage of their offers, though. He hadn't indulged his passions since the Banshee. And as they turned up their noses when he passed, he suspected he would never have to deflect their attentions again. He felt little loss there. Ever since bedding the Banshee he kept his passions in check.

Their whispers reached him. Deliberately, he suspected. He heard the word "devil" and resisted the urge to wrap his fingers around their slender white necks. That these people whom he had known his whole life would all so easily condemn Devlin caused his anger to surge. His hands fisted at his sides.

"Ho, MacDonald!" the butcher called.

Patrick gave an impatient wave. No more. He continued on.

As he neared the house he could hear a thumping sound coming from deep within. He entered, finding a worried Mrs. O'Grady in the drawing room.

"Oh, I'm glad ya' be home, Master Patrick," she said.

Again, a thump came from the back bedroom and they both turned toward the sound.

"What is it, Mrs. O'Grady?" His heart started to pound as it had last night. "Is Devlin all right?"

The woman's brow furrowed. "He looks all right," she stated. "But I can't reach him."

Patrick ran to the room, finding a mess of linens and books and papers littering the floor. Devlin stood in one corner, banging his little body against the wall again and again.

"Devlin!" Patrick shouted.

The child gave no sign of response, just continued to crash himself into the wall. Patrick felt each impact himself.

"He made this mess, Master Patrick," Mrs. O'Grady said behind him. "Like a wild thing. And then he began to… to…"

"It's all right," Patrick said. He stepped toward the child. Red marks already marred the fair skin of his arms and legs. "Devlin. Stop that."

The boy froze for a second, then began his self-abuse again. Patrick grabbed him, holding tight as the boy kicked and writhed in his arms. Devlin's eyes were wild, as if lit by a fire Patrick could almost feel.

"Easy, Devlin," he soothed. "Easy, son."

In the next instant the boy went limp, scaring Patrick witless. He looked the child over, taking in the vacant eyes and the lack of expression, but could find no cause for the change.

Patrick sat on the floor then, cradling the child in his lap. He rocked him the way he'd seen Luke soothe Bryce after some minor injury or other. He prayed the movement would soothe him.

"Easy, Devlin," he said again.

Patrick dropped a kiss on the child's silky curls, and the show of affection remarkably came natural to him. Devlin moved against him, slow and tentative. Burrowing against Patrick's chest, the child let out a sigh and Patrick felt himself ease.

"I'll leave ya', Master Patrick," Mrs. O'Grady said.

Patrick just nodded, holding his son close to his heart.

"I want to help you, son," he whispered. "Pray, tell me how to help you."

The child said nothing, just kept his face tight against Patrick's chest. Patrick closed his eyes and felt one hot tear trickle from beneath his lashes. Never in his life had he felt so utterly helpless.

Chapter 3

"I can't thank you enough, Brianna."

"Devlin is family, Patrick." Luke's wife smiled as she walked into the living room. "As much as Bryce."

"That's not what the people of the dell believe," Patrick sneered, the anger still fresh. "Surely your ears caught the evil they're spreading."

"Don't let their words hurt you, Patrick." Brianna placed her hands on her hips, lifting her chin with determination. "Or Devlin."

Patrick could almost feel the magic the Pixie possessed in her small frame. Positive energy radiated from her and lifted his own spirits.

"Now where is my nephew?" she asked with a nod.

Patrick showed her to his room, and to the little boy sitting like a statue in the corner.

"He used to sleep on the floor," he explained. "I found him there a few times last night and had to put him back up on the bed."

Brianna nodded again and stepped closer to Devlin. "What a beautiful boy, Patrick." She glanced at Patrick and smiled softly. "He looks just like you."

35

She knelt before Devlin, arranging her skirts around her as she folded her hands in her lap. "Hello, Devlin. I'm your Aunt Brianna."

Patrick held his breath, praying for some response from his son. Brianna murmured something under her breath and her hair began to move by an unseen breeze. As she held up her hands and brought them closer together, Patrick saw a flash of blue arc between her palms. Brianna placed her hands near Devlin's cheeks, pressing the blue current toward him until his little face was submerged in it. Devlin gave a start and fixed his gaze on Brianna's. In the next instant Brianna jerked back from him, landing on her bottom.

Alarmed, Patrick ran to her but she waved his concerns aside.

"I'm all right," she insisted. She pulled in a breath. "I can't reach him, Patrick," she whispered. "I'm so sorry."

Devlin went back to staring at the floor, as still as a statue once more.

"But you made a connection, Brianna," Patrick said. "I saw it."

"Not with Devlin," she said. "I couldn't. Something is

36

blocking his mind."

Patrick's heart sank. "Banshee magic."

"Maybe." Brianna ran a hand over her hair. "I… I don't know. And I'm afraid to use stronger magic on him. He's such a little thing."

Patrick spared his son another glance and nodded.

"Aye." He bent down to Devlin. "I'll be right outside, son. I need to talk to Aunt Brianna."

Brianna's eyes were shiny but Patrick kept his own despair in check.

"I don't know how much he understands," Patrick said as they entered the drawing room. "Is there nothing you can do?"

"I don't know anything about troubled children, Patrick."

"But, when Violet was ill you found a way to heal her."

"My sister had a medical problem," she said. "A blood disorder. Devlin's problems are much more delicate. Elusive."

Something occurred to Patrick, something he hadn't yet considered.

"But future medicine helped Violet," he said.

Brianna nodded, then gave him a questioning look. "Patrick, what are you thinking?"

"Thank you again, Brianna."

"Patrick?" she asked again.

"It's nothing," he said.

Brianna stopped in front of the open door. "Call me if you need anything?"

"Aye," he said quickly. He ushered her out the door, eager to puzzle out the notion taking root in his mind. Future medicine had healed the Pixie's sister. Perhaps there was a chance he could find help for Devlin in the future, too.

That night, Patrick sat on the edge of his bed. He eyed the small pallet bed set against one wall, closely watching the little form curled upon it.

Devlin began to toss and turn, kicking at the blankets and flailing his fists in the air. His face bore evidence of a nightmare Patrick feared would rival his own. God, he wouldn't wish such a fate on his worst enemy.

Patrick rose and approached the little bed. "Forgive me, son," he said softly.

A soft sobbing met his ears as Devlin sat up. His eyes snapped open, pinning Patrick with their blue gaze. Devlin reached out and took Patrick's hand, sending a spark up his arm.

"Devlin," Patrick gasped.

The boy just stared at him, his mouth moving soundlessly. Patrick could feel it, a plea to free the boy from his penance. *Ah, God.* Devlin shouldn't have to pay for his father's sin.

"What is it, son?" Patrick sat on the pallet beside him, still holding tight to his hand. "Pray, tell me."

The boy blinked, his gaze suddenly as clear as water. No tears showed on his smooth cheeks, but the anguish in his eyes cut Patrick deeply. He hugged Devlin as he had that afternoon and, after a heart-stopping moment, the boy relaxed against his chest.

"I will fix this, Devlin." Patrick cried the tears his son couldn't, his own cheeks wet as he cradled his son. "You won't pay for my sin any longer. I make you my promise."

***

Patrick stood in the clearing, his hand clutching the amber tied around his neck. He pushed aside a touch of guilt as he fingered the coin-sized slice of stone. Surely his uncle wouldn't miss the talisman for the short time Patrick would be gone. He wore Luke's future clothes, too. Breeches of rough blue fabric and a soft shirt of tartan plaid. On his feet he wore the most surprisingly comfortable shoes. Painted leather topping thick soles that felt like a featherbed. If his journey went as he hoped, he would have his family's belongings back to them before they discovered them missing.

He closed his eyes and imagined the place Luke had found his Pixie. The amber began to warm against his palm. A sound filled his ears, like howling wind or rushing water. The ground tilted beneath his feet and then... silence. A moment later he fell on his backside. Hard. He released the amber and braced his hands behind him.

The ground was rough beneath his palms, with none of the clearing's soft grass. Cautiously, he opened his eyes and found he sat on a walk made of what felt like limestone. People walking past him shot him odd looks, and he guessed he shouldn't be sitting right there.

Giving a slight groan, he stood and rolled his shoulders. As he stepped over to the brick building closest to him, he refrained from rubbing his backside in clear view of these "now" people.

Patrick leaned against the building, his eyes darting from one wonder to the next. Carriages and wagons—cars and trucks, his brother had told him—made their noisy way up and down the wide street. They were as loud and noxious-smelling as Luke had said, and Patrick would no longer wonder if Luke made up the tales of this Indianapolis.

The people here looked much like those in the dell, though. Aside from their dress, that was. Some of the men wore comfortable clothes like he did. Others wore jackets with matching breeches and long, thin neck cloths. They all seemed to be in a hurry.

"Excuse me," a breathy, female voice said from behind him.

Patrick saw that he blocked the entrance to the building at his back and stepped away to allow the woman to pass. She flipped her long, golden hair and gazed at him over one shoulder. To his surprise her eyes held an offer he'd seen many times before. Lord, his charm worked on mortal women! This was a complication he didn't need.

"Pray, forgive me," he said as he stepped further away from her.

She stared at him, her eyes slightly out of focus, and ran a hand over her short skirt. Toying with its hem, she smiled. "No problem."

Patrick held himself still. After a long moment she walked past him, no doubt swaying her slender hips for his attention. Patrick dismissed her from his mind in the next instant. Even if he weren't in such a hurry to find help for Devlin he wouldn't make such ill use of a woman. But it would take a tight rein to keep his charm in check. The time jump must have jarred his control.

He glanced up and down the busy street, trying to get his bearings in the strange place. MacDonald Braunachs were cunning, but even his sharp mind couldn't figure out the location of the healing place without some help. He knew it was called the Children's Hospital, from Luke and Brianna's tales. That was the place he sought. But, where was it?

He nodded absently at another woman who looked him up and down. He could no doubt charm one of the women here into telling him. He stepped closer to her and her lips parted. But he wouldn't dare risk the inevitable side effect. The scar high on his back began to throb and he shook his head. A sexual dalliance wasn't to anyone's advantage.

He began to walk down the sidewalk, keeping well away from the smelly and crowded roadway, and tried to find someone to help him in his quest. It was morning here as it had been in the clearing, and the weather was similar to that he left behind. It was spring here in Indianapolis too, then.

A tall thick man in a dark blue uniform with the look of authority about him stood on the nearest corner. A constable, perhaps? Surely he would be the one to help Patrick.

He stepped toward the man. "Pardon me, sir?"

The dark-haired man turned and ran his eyes over Patrick. Apparently Patrick passed the unknown test, for the constable visibly relaxed and nodded.

"Yeah?" he asked.

"I need the location of the Children's Hospital, please."

The man arched a thick brow. "It's north of the city, pal. Up Meridian."

With such tall buildings around him, Patrick couldn't guess which way was north. And he had no idea what "meridian" the man spoke of.

"I don't know how to find north," he admitted.

"Look, buddy. Get on the bus over there and it'll take you up to the hospital." He nodded and smiled at last. "Just watch for the stops."

Patrick blinked. Bus? He opened his mouth to ask another question but the constable had already turned his attention to a small group of adolescents laughing and rough-housing on the other side of the street. They wore torn and baggy pants and

Patrick was surprised to see their drawers peeping from above the waistbands. He turned back to the constable to ask what, precisely, a "bus" was, but the lawman was already on his way to halt the young men's antics.

Patrick looked to where the man had indicated, finding a few benches set near a wider expanse of street. Thankfully, he wouldn't have to cross the thoroughfare to reach it. He made his way toward the benches, reading the signs along the sidewalk. When he reached the "bus stop" he was relieved to find a map within, along with a sign listing several stops.

"It must be like a post carriage," he said.

He gave a start and glanced around, pleased to find no one within hearing. He'd have to watch himself. It wouldn't do for some mortal to find him peculiar. They might call the constable and delay Patrick's quest. He would brook no such delay. Not when Devlin was depending on him.

He sat on the bench, watching the people who passed by as he waited for the bus. More than one woman eyed him as the others had and he fought to keep a look of disinterest on his face.

A roar louder than any of the cars he'd seen so far

brought a large vehicle toward him. He gulped and came to his feet. The carriage was huge, with sunlight glinting off its wide silver front as it groaned and wheezed to a stop. With a squeak and whoosh, the door opened and he steeled himself. He stepped up onto the bus, ignoring a stench like burning peat. The driver nodded to him. Patrick pulled out a piece of future money and handed it to the driver.

He eyed the bill. "Where you goin'? Canada?"

Patrick shook his head and smiled. A bit of charm would keep the man from thinking him daft.

"How much to go to the Children's Hospital?" he asked.

The man blinked, and then returned his smile. "Two bucks'll get you that far. I'll let you know when we get close to yer stop."

Patrick found two notes with the numeral one on them and handed them over. "I thank you."

As he moved to take a seat, the bus lurched to life. He clutched at the nearest railing, holding his breath as the vehicle swayed from side to side. He made his way to the nearest vacant seat and settled back, ignoring the mortals around him.

The horrid smell was faint with the vehicle's door closed, but it still stung his nostrils. To ease his roiling stomach, he

45

looked out the window.

As they traveled north of the city, more green grass could be seen. Spring-waking trees stood along the road, and he began to think the city was rather pretty. The bus made a few jerking stops, and people got on and off with looks of purpose on their faces. He held on to the seat.

Soon he accustomed himself to the rocking motion and looked about the bus. His gaze settled on a young mortal woman seated across from him. She was a pretty little thing, with long sable hair tied back to swing free to her shoulders. A ponytail, he knew from Brianna. His sister-in-law favored the same style. This girl wore breeches as well, like Brianna often did.

She held a thick book in her lap, and pored over the contents with a slight frown on her brow. Patrick watched her, eyeing her rosy lips as she mouthed one word or other to herself. He tried to read the book's title, but couldn't as the cover pressed against her knees.

He opened his mouth to ask about her book, closing it with a snap in the next instant. He wouldn't engage a mortal woman in conversation. He already felt a pull toward the pretty girl, watching as she sat so gracefully with her ponytail gently swaying with the bus's motion. With his nerves in such a raw state from Devlin's trouble and the time jump to this strange world, he suspected his charm would be out of his control with a woman he found attractive. But as she tucked a loose strand of hair behind one shell-like ear, he acknowledged the attraction to himself at least. She fingered the corner of the page before she turned it, stroking the edge with the tip.

"Children's Hospital," the driver called.

Patrick straightened and shook off his contemplation. He hid his smile as the pretty girl shot the driver a look of surprise. Apparently his charm ensured such preferential treatment from the driver, since no other stops had been called during the ride. Shrugging her slight shoulders, she gathered up her books and a large pack. Patrick glanced out the window as the bus stopped and saw a large sign that confirmed the driver's words.

Relieved, he stood. The girl stilled across from him as he faced her, and then her eyes ran slowly over his form. To his dismay, her interest didn't fill him with dread. Instead heat flooded him and he leaned away from her. She gave him a small smile, just a slight curve of her full lips, but he felt it more keenly than the woman who'd eyed him hungrily on the street earlier.

When this girl stood and hurried off the bus, he was oddly relieved. But he had to follow her lead, at last stopping to stare up at the massive building as the girl disappeared from his view. The bus door slammed shut behind him and the vehicle squealed and roared as it continued up the street.

Patrick walked slowly up to the large glass doors, staring at his puzzled reflection as he looked for a handle. To his astonishment the doors slid open as soon as he stepped closer. With a touch of hope, he realized this place wasn't without its own magic.

Chairs filled seating areas in the very large lobby, but otherwise the inside of the hospital confused him. Signs bearing words he had never read hung on the walls, with arrows directing people one way or the other. He spied a large desk set against one wall and recognized the word above it: information. The old woman behind the counter smiled when he walked up to her, which he decided to take as a sign his luck might be about to change.

"Hello, Madam," he began with a grin. "I need a bit of help."

***

Tara Connor closed her textbook and donned the white lab coat hanging in her locker. She put the book on the stack set on the top shelf and let out a breath. With just a few more credits she'd finally be able to leave the books behind.

She peered into the mirror on her locker door, tucking one strand of hair that had come loose from her ponytail. She wore no makeup this morning. She sighed. She'd had no time, really. She stashed her backpack in the locker and closed the door.

As she headed for the behavior lab, she reviewed the cases she'd read about most recently. The kids in the lab, her kids, brought by parents desperate for the latest techniques in reaching them, challenged her mind and her heart. Mostly suffering from different degrees of Autism, the children built walls around themselves. Tara considered it her calling to breach those walls, and she'd gladly used all the financial aid she'd earned and the grant money she'd won to find a way to reunite these kids with their parents. It was a pity she'd had no way to reach her own.

"Good morning, Miss Connor," a passing nurse called with a smile.

Tara smiled her own greeting and pushed open the swinging door leading to the lab. Already four children waited just outside the glass-enclosed playroom, their still bodies and blank faces a testament to the reason for their visit. She once more felt that determination fill her.

"Hello, Miss Connor," one of the mother's said.

The woman's red-rimmed eyes held hope that touched Tara's heart. The little girl at her side, Chelsea, said nothing and made no expression of recognition in Tara's direction.

"Hello, Chelsea." With a bright smile, Tara opened the door to the playroom and the grown-ups ushered in the children. Chelsea and the others took halting steps, but let their parents direct them for now.

Tara sucked in a breath, harnessing all of her spirit, knowledge and hope, and entered the playroom herself.

***

Patrick at last found the place the old woman had told him of, the "lab" where children with such problems as Devlin came for help. He prayed there was some elixir here to right their injured minds, and that it would work on his son. Last night he'd held Devlin in his arms and made him his promise. He would sooner die than go back on his word.

He began to search for some indication of a medicine that would work, vowing he would gladly steal any opportunity to give the boy a chance at a real life.

50

This smaller place didn't seem as daunting as the entrance to the hospital. Here the walls were painted with lively characters, like rabbits and mice and flowers. Brightly-colored chairs both large and child-sized lined the walls, and there was less of that stinging smell he'd encountered in the hallways. He looked around, trying to fathom where to begin to find his answers.

Through a glass wall he saw what looked like a nursery. Balls and dolls and blocks littered the floor which was covered with a shiny soft-looking padding. There were a few children within. Some appeared older than Devlin and others just his age. One boy rocked back and forth as Devlin often did, his eyes staring straight ahead. Another threw blocks at the wall, a fierce frown on his face. Patrick watched one pretty little girl stare openmouthed at nothing. He recognized that blankness. Chilled, he looked away.

To his left he saw a rack holding glossy leaflets. He selected a few, trying to make sense of the words and initials standing for things he'd never heard of. Lists of symptoms caught his eye, but he couldn't find any "syndrome" that completely described Devlin's particular trouble. His shoulders slumped and he gazed through the glass once more.

He saw her then, the lovely young woman from the bus. She

stood off to one side of the nursery, speaking to a woman who must be the mother of one of the children. The mother's face was haggard with worry, but the younger woman's demeanor seemed to ease her. She wore an overcoat of white, as he had seen some of the doctors here wear. Was she a doctor, then?

He stepped over to the glass and watched closely as she approached the vacant little girl. She eased down on the floor beside her and flashed an easy, pretty smile. The child didn't react but just continued to stare at nothing. The young woman persisted, edging closer to the little girl as her mouth continued to move. Patrick couldn't hear through the glass, but by her stance and expression he was amazed that the child could ignore such a compelling presence. He couldn't make himself look away. The concern in her eyes, the welcoming in her posture, drew him.

At last he saw it, a flicker of something in the child's blank eyes. If he hadn't been watching so closely, he would have missed the tiny motion of the little girl as she leaned a fraction closer to the young woman. A smile curved one corner of her slack mouth, earning obvious praise from the woman. She ruffled the child's golden curls and dropped a kiss on her brow. Ah. Patrick knew the reason she could reach the child. She was magic.

Patrick glanced at the leaflets once more and gave a shake of his head. The papers wouldn't help Devlin. Printed words couldn't help Patrick reach his son as the young woman had reached the little girl behind the glass. He didn't need anything here in Indianapolis. Nay. He needed the young woman's magic.

Patrick stared once more through the glass. There was only one solution. He would take her back to Meath Province. He would take her to Devlin.

Chapter 4

Tara sat back on her heels, her heart lifting to see Chelsea's progress. Three days a week over the last two months she had worked with the child, in accordance with the instructions of Chelsea's doctor. And the spark of life in the little girl's eyes gave her a cautious hope that there was a way to bring the child completely back to her parents. After seeing that one of the undergraduate volunteers watched over the children in the playroom, Tara stood. Eager to update her notes, she stepped into the hallway.

She saw him then, the good-looking man from the bus. She took a moment to appreciate the way his jeans hugged his long legs, and the way his flannel shirt spanned the breadth of his shoulders. He stood near the rack of pamphlets, confusion etched on his face, and ran a frustrated hand over his strawberry-gold curls.

She stepped toward him. "May I help you?"

He turned to face her fully, and she stared up into crystal blue eyes. "Aye." He flashed a gorgeous smile. "I daresay I'm at a bit of a loss here."

He spoke in an accent she couldn't quite place. British, maybe. Or Irish. The image of the hunk in the soap

commercials struck her, fresh and strong. *Manly, yes.* She shook
her head to clear it.

"I'm Tara Connor," she said. "An assistant here in the
Behavior Lab."

He nodded, light shining off his curls, and she blinked. He
truly was gorgeous.

"Have you always cared for children, then?" he asked.

"Yes," she answered without question.

"Why?" he asked with another smile.

She opened her mouth to berate him for prying, but instead
found herself smiling in response to his grin. It was suddenly so
warm in here. She reached up to widened the V in her lab coat.

"I have no parents," she said. "No family, really. And these
children..." She swallowed. "They're locked away from their
parents by their afflictions."

He stepped closer to her, giving a slow nod.

"How do you help them?" he coaxed.

"I..." She gasped, suddenly even warmer. "I work with
them, study their symptoms. When I break through those walls?
Oh, there's nothing like it."

He reached out to touch her hand, and she felt heat spread
through her body. She breathed in, smelling the clean scent of

him, and her pulse pounded.

"You are special, Tara Connor," he said. "Aye, that's true."

***

Patrick watched the young woman, certain he held her in his lure. Her cheeks blushed a pretty pink, and her amber eyes were wide and slightly out of focus. One delicate hand rubbed the base of her throat as she breathed through parted lips.

He asked her a few more questions, easily gaining all the answers he needed. He knew she was wise in the ways of these poor children. She was the one to help Devlin. Stepping back, he released her from his charm.

Obviously still a bit flustered, the girl tucked a loose lock of her thick sable hair behind one ear. She nodded and walked to the glassed-in area, stopping as she placed her hand on the door. That glance over one shoulder showed him all, her confusion and her wariness. Guilt niggled at him but he shut it out. He didn't need the medical advances of this time as Brianna's sister had. Nay. He needed the knowledge in Tara's mind. As she turned away and reentered the lab, he felt a smile curve his lips.

***

Tara placed her backpack on the counter and crossed to the stout fridge set in one corner of her kitchenette. She withdrew a can of diet soda and popped the tab, relishing the hiss of air as the drink gave off its promise of cool refreshment. Feeling drained, she looked forward to the shot of caffeine.

She took a bubbly sip of soda and perched on one of the stools bracketing the kitchen. Her small apartment near the campus of the downtown university was nothing fancy, but it suited her. She didn't have a roommate, and her schedule was her own. She placed the soda can on the chipped counter and dropped her chin in her hands. There was no one to question her lack of a social life. That was for sure.

Her work was challenging, and she didn't need to remind herself of this since little Chelsea had been the only child to show any sign of improvement all day. Slowly, so very slowly, these children made their way through the milestones that represented their development. Though the odds were steep, Tara prayed that each of these children would someday master complex communication and form total attachment to their parents and surroundings.

After the handsome man had left the behavior lab, she'd

been able to focus fully on her work. But when he'd been there?

She recalled little of their conversation in the hallway, just the pleasant glow she'd felt as he asked her about her work. His eyes were the most amazing shade of blue she'd ever seen, like fresh dew on a violet or something romantic like that. Her hand still tingled with the memory of his touch, which was both strong and gentle. And his body wasn't bad, either.

Tara stood and crossed to the fridge again, pulled a frozen dinner out of the freezer and popped it into the microwave. The scent of tomato sauce and hot cardboard filled the kitchen and as the microwave hummed she clicked on the TV with the remote and flipped through the channels.

It took little time to down her meager meal and clean up after herself. She turned off the light in the kitchen and went into the living room. She barely glanced at the blank walls, since no family photos hung there as usual. There were no baby pictures either. Her mother never had much time for picture taking when she was straight, not that Tara could remember many times when the woman wasn't high. She'd overdosed when Tara was four years old, and there had been no father around and no friends to see to Tara or her childhood remembrances. No one had cared enough to take any photos after she'd ended up at children's services, either.

Year after lonely year, hope after dashed hope, had left her in the dedicated care of those paid for their attention. At least the folks running that last foster home had encouraged her studies, helping with state contests for scholarships and awards for academic excellence.

She reached up and pulled out her ponytail holder, letting her thick hair free. Sighing, she put her feet up on the coffee table and reached for the TV remote again.

A knock came at the door. She eyed the door, puzzled. No one ever visited. And the best thing about her apartment building was that there was no soliciting allowed.

"Maybe it's the manager," she said to herself. She flicked off the TV and rose to cross to the door.

She peered through the peephole, shocked to see the man from the behavior lab standing there. How had he found her? Almost as if she couldn't help herself, she opened the door, but not before sliding the security chain loudly into place.

"Yes?"

"I need you, Tara."

Her hand trembled on the door knob as he caught her with his gaze. He smiled and that warmth spread through her again. Her heart began to pound with anticipation. As if of its own accord, her hand released the chain and she opened the door.

One of his strong hands gripped something hanging on a strip of leather around his neck, and she thought she saw light peeking from between his clenched fingers. His expression was grave now, his face no longer wearing that teasing grin.

She blinked as he stepped into the apartment and closed the door, suddenly cold. "Hey, I didn't say you could—"

"You must come with me, Tara."

He grabbed her arm but before she could manage more than an aborted cry, the room began to spin. Her ears rang from the roaring sound and her head spun with vertigo as her stomach threatened to heave up her frozen dinner. His grip never faltered, though. He held her tight as she felt the world go dark and silent.

The floor came up to meet her and she tried to suck in a breath. She slowly opened her eyes, staring up at the pink sky above her. The wind had nearly been knocked out of her, so she gasped and tried to move. The man's big body was on top of her, though he quickly remedied that.

"Forgive me," he said, easing off of her.

She leaned up on her elbows, her fingers clenching in the cool grass beneath her. *Grass?* What the hell? Looking around, she saw nothing but trees. And the man. He stood above her, a worried frown on his face.

He held out his hand to her. "Are you all right, Tara?"

Damn him and his chivalry, anyway. She pushed away his offered hand and stood. "Where the hell are we?"

"My home."

"Your home? You abducted me? I'll call the police. You can't just come and take women from their homes to satisfy your... your..."

She couldn't finish the thought, could hardly catch her breath after falling here in the woods.

"I need your help."

She brushed off her jeans and placed her hands on her hips. "Listen, Mr... What's your name?"

"I'm Patrick MacDonald."

She ignored the gallant tip of his head.

"Well, Patrick MacDonald. Take me home right now."

"I can't, lass."

She turned around then, seeing nothing familiar about the woods. She'd learned about self-defense, and recalled that once taken by a killer a woman's chances for survival dramatically decreased. Secondary murder scene, or something like that. She turned to face him, backing away slowly.

Would he kill her and leave her body for the raccoons? She eyed him. She didn't sense anything so vile about him. In fact he seemed deferential at the moment. Cordial, even.

"Well, I'm going home," she told him.

With a bravery she hoped would fool him she stomped toward the sunset. She prayed it would lead her back to Indianapolis. He grabbed her wrist in a flash and held on tight.

"You can't walk home, Tara."

Wrenching her wrist out of his grasp, she asked, "Why the hell not?"

"We're in Ireland."

She stared hard at him. "Ireland? Listen, Patrick MacDonald. I don't know what your game is—"

"It's no game, Tara." He raked his fingers through his

hair, a show of frustration she could understand. "It's important you stay here."

She quirked a brow at him. "In Ireland?"

He smiled. "Aye. Meath Province, to be precise."

She rubbed her hands over her face. "O-kay"

"There's more."

She slanted him a look. "Gee, why did I think there wouldn't be?"

He held on to her shoulders and for the first time in this ridiculous exchange she felt fear. Real fear, not of murderous captors or crazed sex fiends. Not of him, but of what he would say. She braced herself.

"You're in my time, Tara," he said. "1814."

That rushing sound came again and then she felt nothing.

***

Patrick caught Tara as she fainted into his arms. He feared the time jump was too much for the lass. It would be easier now to take her to the dell, though. And she wasn't eyeing him with that combination of pique and fear. He scooped her into his arms and carried her home.

He brought her to Luke and Brianna's, thinking it was the best place for her at present. He hadn't asked her to see to Devlin yet, and surely his uncle wouldn't be pleased to learn Patrick had made use of the amber without his permission. There would more than enough time for that scolding later.

He gazed down at the woman in his arms. There was nothing to her, yet she was curved in all the right places. Her hair, free of its ponytail, brushed over his arm. Thick and silky-smooth, the mass tempted him to run his fingers through it. Her smooth cheeks were pale though, and guilt slashed through him. No matter. The girl was strong, in spirit and body. She would weather this challenge. Hadn't she clearly stated her wishes back there in the woods?

A smile tugged at his lips. Aye, she was pretty in her ire. All trembling and rosy. But her appeal didn't matter. Devlin was the reason for all of this. And he prayed that when she met the little boy her heart and dedication wouldn't allow her to leave.

He came to Luke's house and shifted Tara in his arms. He knocked on the door, shifting from foot to foot as he waited for an answer. Brianna opened the door, her smile of greeting swiftly changing to an expression of surprise.

"Patrick! Who is this?"

"Pray let me in, Brianna."

She stepped aside and closed the door behind him.

"Patrick." She braced her hands on her hips. "What have you done?"

"She's from your time, Brianna. And when I told her where and when she was now, she fainted."

Brianna's blue eyes widened. "You took her? My God, how?"

"That's of little consequence now. Pray, see to her?"

To his relief, Brianna nodded. "Yes, yes. Bring her into Bryce's room."

Patrick turned down the hallway. "Where's Luke?" he called over his shoulder.

"He took Bryce for a walk after dinner," came her answer from right behind him.

Patrick nodded and laid Tara on the narrow bed. He brushed her hair out of her face and ran his finger over one cool cheek.

"I need her, Brianna." He faced his sister-in-law. "For Devlin."

Brianna said nothing, her brow furrowed in question. Patrick straightened and gave her a nod.

"She's Tara Connor, from Indianapolis."

Brianna's eyes widened again but she said nothing this time.

65

He left the room, knowing Tara was in good hands.

As he entered the living room his brother Luke came home. He was preceded by a bundle of energy who could only be Bryce. When the boy saw Patrick, he stopped in his tracks. In the next instant he launched himself at him.

"Uncle Patrick!" he squealed.

Patrick bent down and lifted the boy in his arms. Bryce gave him a noisy kiss and hugged him tight. Patrick's heart clenched. He was so different from Devlin.

He kissed Bryce on the cheek and set him on his feet. "Good to see you, Bryce."

The little boy beamed a smile. "Mama and Papa and me went to London."

"Just now?" Patrick teased.

"Nay!" Bryce giggled. "Papa took me for a walk just now."

"And did you have a good time, then?"

"Aye." He eyed Patrick's clothes. "Why are you dressed like Papa does sometimes?"

"Your Mama's waitin' for you," he said, ignoring the boy's question.

Bryce nodded and ran down the hallway.

Patrick stood and faced his brother. "Hello, Luke."

"How are you, brother?" Luke looked at him with concern. "How's the boy?"

Patrick shook his head. "He's not well. But I think I found a way to—"

"Papa!" Bryce ran back into the room. "There's a lady in my bed!"

Patrick felt his face flush as Luke stared at him.

"I have something to tell you, Luke."

Luke reached down to ruffle Bryce's auburn curls. "Go see your Mama, son." He shot a look of meaning at Patrick. "Your uncle has something to tell me."

Bryce nodded and skipped back down the hallway.

"Now, Luke—"

"What did you do, Patrick?"

Patrick swallowed. "I took Uncle's amber and went to Indianapolis."

Luke snorted. "That explains why you be wearin' my clothes. Why?"

"I had to find help for Devlin. I promised him."

Luke shook his head and paced the length of the room. "You went to the future." He rubbed the back of his neck. "And you took a woman?"

"Aye, but not just any woman. She's gifted, Luke. She works with children like Devlin. Well, not precisely like Devlin."

Luke stopped pacing and faced him. "But you took a woman from the future against her will?"

Patrick nodded, his fists clenched. "Aye. And I'd do it again to give my son the chance at a real life!"

Patrick slumped onto the settee beside the hearth and buried his face in his hands, the fight in him gone as soon as it came.

"Tell me, brother," Luke said in a low voice.

"You didn't see him, Luke," Patrick said. "The boy begged me to help him."

He could hear Luke's footsteps as he approached. "Devlin spoke to you?"

"Nay. If only he would." He raised his head to face his brother. "But I know what he wants. His poor tortured heart spoke to me." He placed his hand on his chest. "Here."

Luke sat down beside him and placed a hand on his shoulder. "You love the boy."

The truth of it wrapped itself around Patrick's heart.

"Aye."

Luke gave his shoulder a squeeze. "He's a lucky boy."

Patrick gave a curt nod and stood. "Pray, keep an eye on the girl? She fainted when we leaped here." A smiled tugged one corner of his mouth. "Well, after she blistered my ears, she fainted. She's a strong lass."

"She's welcome here," Luke said.

"Patrick," Brianna said from the hallway.

Patrick looked at her. "Aye?"

"She's coming around."

Patrick wanted to run to Tara's side, to convince her to stay and help Devlin. He was selfish to wish he could make her see reason tonight, after all he'd put her through.

"Well, she won't want to see me at present." Patrick stood. "I'll be back in the morning."

Before Brianna could add her protests to Tara's, Patrick left the cottage for home. That night the Banshee came to Patrick in his nightmares, as vague and as sharp as that first night of his sin.

"Aye, Patrick," the Banshee cooed. "Make me scream…"

Patrick stood stock still as the witch ran her hands over the front of him. His shirt fluttered to the ground behind him and she began to work the buttons of his breeches free. She was beautiful as she smiled up at him, her violet eyes sparkling and her teeth gleaming straight and even. Her skin was smooth and luminous, and if she didn't have her hand curved around his shaft he could almost imagine her an angel.

"Nay," he said, his voice lacking any conviction as she stroked him. His pulse pounded in his ears as his erection grew heavy.

With a laugh low in her throat, the witch stretched out on the fog-shrouded ground. Beckoning to him, she bent her legs until her gossamer dress fell back to reveal her belly and the fair hair shielding her center. Patrick stared for a long moment, his mind urging him to flee even as his body surged him forward.

"Come, Braunach," she whispered.

Patrick fell on her, drove into her as she clutched at him. He could feel nothing but her body grasping him deep within her, drawing him deeper into her unholy heat. Tighter and tighter she pulled, and Patrick felt his soul mixing with her black one. Vile thoughts slithered into his mind, selfish thoughts of conquest and triumph, and his belly churned.

He knew his release was close, could feel his body tightening, and leaned back on his arms. "Nay, witch!"

She laughed, the sound like sharp nails across his brain. "Aye, Patrick."

She wrapped her arms around him, holding tight to his back as he began to lose control. He could feel the burning start, high up on his left shoulder blade. Tingling, itching, his skin felt like it was on fire. Her fingers branded him and he roared, his control gone as he spilled his seed deep and high within her.

Patrick sat up, his hand tight over his mouth as he fought the nausea roiling in his belly. Devlin still slept, his face wearing a frown from his nest of blankets on the floor. Patrick stood on shaking legs and then he lifted his son back up on the small pallet. Aye, he looked like a MacDonald. But Patrick couldn't ignore the features he'd inherited from his mother.

He went back to the bed, careful not to roll over onto his back, onto his scar. God, he'd been so weak. He'd let the witch lead him into darkness and he'd dumbly followed. That first night was the only one of any clarity in his memory. He knew that those two weeks had been full of their coupling, in every way he'd ever imagined and some he hadn't from his limited experience with the seasoned harlots of the dell. He curled on his side, his arms wrapped around his belly as he prayed.

Forgive me, God. Forgive me, Devlin.

Chapter 5

Tara heard a child's voice, the sound sweet and inquisitive, and shifted on the sweet-smelling sheets.

"Who is she, Mama?" the voice asked.

Was she was back at the behavior lab? That couldn't be right. Despite the fact her entire body still felt like it was sleeping, her mind reasoned that none of those children ever spoke so clearly. She stirred and shifted, the sheets rustling beneath her as they gave up their fresh lavender scent. She froze. Lavender?

"Tara." An adult voice, this one feminine and soft, reached through to her. "Tara, are you awake?"

Her eyes snapped open and she stared up at the unfamiliar coffered ceiling. Light from an oil lamp beside the bed flickered over the walls. No, she wasn't in the behavior lab. Where was she?

"Tara?" the woman asked again.

Tara blinked and focused on the pretty blond woman sitting beside her as the rest of the room slowly swam into focus. Crisp primary colors dressed the walls, matching the bedding that Tara nervously clutched in her hands. "Y-yes?"

The woman, Tara guessed she was near her own age,

smiled. "Good evening."

Tara ran a hand over rumpled clothes and hesitantly returned the expression. "Where am I?"

A little boy with glossy reddish curls peeped around the woman, his blue eyes round. "You're in Ireland!"

The woman clicked her tongue. "Bryce, please." She eased the boy off of the bed. "Go see your Papa." After the boy withdrew to a spot a few feet from the bed, the woman smiled at Tara again. "Hello, Tara. I'm Brianna MacDonald."

"MacDonald." Tara leaned up on her elbows, her fogged mind trying to make sense of this. It struck her then, the reason the name was familiar to her. "Oh! The man who brought me here?"

The woman nodded. "Yes, Tara. He's my brother-in-law. Patrick MacDonald."

Tara nodded absently. Her brother-in-law. Tara glanced at this woman, Brianna. She seemed kind, and by her accent Tara guessed her to be British. She was dressed like something out of a PBS production of Jane Austen though, and her hair was coiled on top of her head. Something struck the back of her mind again, something from last night.

Patrick MacDonald had said something about 1814? Her head began to pound.

"This isn't right," Tara said. "I want to go home."

Brianna shook her head. "I'm afraid you'll have to speak to Patrick about that."

"Patrick MacDonald. That man." Tara snorted. "He… he took me from my home."

Brianna nodded at that. "I know. I'm sorry."

Tara blinked. "That's it?" She sat up straighter and flicked her tangled hair out of her eyes. "You're sorry?"

Brianna stood. "You're welcome to stay here. Patrick will be back tomorrow."

The woman said nothing more, and Tara didn't know what she could say that would help her make any sense of this.

She looked around the room. It was obviously a child's bedroom, decorated with bright colors and simple, sturdy furniture. There were no lights in the room but the oil lamp though, not in the ceiling and not visible in the hallway. She glanced at Brianna's dress once more as she neared the doorway. 1814, Patrick MacDonald had told her. Could that be true?

"Brianna, wait," Tara called.

The woman stilled, one hand braced on the doorframe.

"Is this really 1814?" Tara asked.

She smiled and nodded.

"Yes." Brianna stepped toward her once more. "I'm not from here either, Tara. I'm from your time."

That pounding started in Tara's head again. "What?"

To Tara's astonishment, Brianna winked. "I'll explain it if you wish, but you've already had a bit of a shock today."

"You're not kidding," Tara muttered.

Brianna's smile widened. "If you're hungry, just let me know. I'll be happy to get you something from the kitchen."

Tara nodded absently and Brianna left. Tara stood and crossed to the window. She couldn't see anything since it was already dark outside. How long had she been asleep? Embarrassment struck her. She must have fainted. Then, how...? Oh God, the man had carried her here? That was just great.

1814, she marveled. Ireland. And Patrick MacDonald would be back for her tomorrow? Well, Mr. tall and handsome had better brace himself. She was going home tomorrow no matter what.

Tara awoke in the narrow bed, surprisingly well-rested despite sleeping in her clothes. The sheets were soft and fine, and the pillow was superior. She didn't know what she'd expected to find in the nineteenth century, but the luxury surprised her.

She rose and stretched. Peering into the mirror on top of the child-sized dresser, she ran her fingers through her tangled hair. She had to use the bathroom, but doubted modern luxury would extend to modern plumbing. She searched her brain, reviewing what little she knew of the nineteenth century. Chamber pots, maybe? Yuck.

Voices came from down the hall, and she recognized one as the little boy she'd met last night. The deeper tone must be the boy's father, though she hadn't seen him yet. And what about Patrick MacDonald? She fumed. Where was that man? The one who dragged her from her home?

She crossed to the door and opened it. The little boy stood there, staring up at her with those huge blue eyes again.

"The lady's awake, Mama!" he shouted.

Tara smiled and crouched down to his level. "Hello. Can you tell me where the... Where the chamber pot is?"

The child laughed and ran back down the hall. "The lady has to use the loo!"

Her cheeks flamed as she stood. The loo? That was British

for bathroom, right? She started. Bathroom?

"Good morning, Tara."

Tara smiled at the blond woman, Brianna. She once more wore a long dress, this one white with little blue flowers.

"Good morning, Brianna."

Brianna leaned closer. "Bryce said you'd like to refresh yourself?"

"Yes, please."

Brianna turned and led her down the hallway to another door. She gave Tara a wink and opened it, showing her a large bathroom with all the comforts of home. Tara gaped at the tiled floor and gleaming tub. And a toilet!

"How…?"

"I admit I bring some of the future back with me every time I visit."

Tara shook her head. "The future?"

Brianna shrugged. "Oh, the dell has its charms." She smiled brightly. "But that's no reason to live without modern conveniences, is it?"

Again, Tara just stared at her. The woman seemed sane and normal, just as she had last night. And yet… In all her studies of psychological disorders Tara had never read of anyone who thought they could travel through time on a whim. She was smack in the middle of a cuckoo clock.

"Th-thank you," Tara nodded.

Brianna let her in the bathroom and closed the door, giving Tara her privacy. Tara opened the lid to the toilet, expecting to see what? she couldn't imagine. There was nothing but clear water in the bowl. "Huh."

She saw to her morning duties and washed her face in the marble sink. Still no lights in here, but lovely sconces stood at the ready with candles when the sunshine didn't come through the window as it did now. Tara raked her fingers through her hair and sighed into the mirror. She opened one of the vanity drawers and found a stash of ribbons. Guessing Brianna wouldn't mind the theft, she withdrew one of pink and gathered her hair into a ponytail.

Birdsongs came through the open window, drawing her to look outside. Last night it had been dark, and that was frightening enough. Now that the sun shone she feared what she would see outside.

Her heart skipping a beat, she pushed aside the lacy curtain and saw nothing strange. Just a lovely view of trees and grass and flowers, and a landscape rich in color. The fresh scent of the air was surprising. Brianna wasn't wrong. This place had its charms indeed.

She left the bathroom and continued down the hall toward what must be the living area of the house. The little boy's chatter reached her first, followed by Brianna's patient responses to his seemingly endless questions. She heard her name mentioned. Little surprise there. She stepped into the kitchen and stood. This room looked modern, as well. Brianna took a pitcher of milk out of the wood-paneled refrigerator and poured a glass for her son.

"Hello," she smiled in Tara's direction.

Tara nodded and came to stand by the wide oak table.

"Hi, Tara," the boy said. "You missed Papa. He went to the workshop. He makes shoes. All the MacDonalds make shoes. I'm Bryce!"

Tara blinked as she sought to process the wealth of information Bryce threw at her.

"Hello, Bryce. Thank you for letting me use your room."

He gave a careless shrug. "I slept with Mama and Papa." He rolled his eyes. "But Papa takes up so much room."

Tara knew that his father was Patrick MacDonald's brother, and no doubt he was as large a man as her abductor. She sat across from Bryce and pondered her next step.

"Would you like some tea, Tara?" Brianna asked.

She perked up at the offer. Caffeine? *Oh, yes.*

"Tea would be great, Brianna. Thank you."

Brianna set a basket of warm scones on the table and Tara took one and began to eat. Tea and cinnamon scones. The scents, the tastes. If she closed her eyes she could almost feel like she was back in her favorite coffee shop back in Indianapolis.

She watched the boy, enchanted by his careful manners as he ate. And by his milk moustache. He grinned at her around a mouthful of scone and she easily smiled back. He was a charmer. She stiffened as she recalled her talk with Patrick at the hospital. Charmer. Just like his uncle.

"Patrick is coming this morning, Tara," Brianna said.

Tara jumped. Could the woman read minds as well as travel to the future?

"Oh. Good. That man…" She snapped her mouth shut as she noticed Bryce's eyes fixed on her. "Never mind."

"I know he took you without your consent."

"He abducted me, Brianna!" Tara calmed herself and took a sip from her cup of very fine tea. "Look. I know he's your brother-in-law. But he kidnapped me."

Bryce clicked his tongue and guilt nagged at her.

"I shouldn't speak ill of your uncle, Bryce," Tara said quickly. "I'm sorry."

"Uncle Patrick would never hurt you, Tara." Bryce looked her square in the eye and she wished she could believe him. "He would never hurt anybody."

Before she could ponder the validity of the boy's assurance, a knock came at the front door. Brianna wiped her hands on a dishtowel and left the kitchen. Tara braced herself, suspecting the visitor would be the man in question.

"Good mornin', Brianna," she heard Patrick say in his now-familiar voice. "Is the girl awake?"

She didn't hear Brianna's reply. She drained her cup of tea and stood, bracing her hands on the sturdy, lovely carved chair. Modern conveniences and quaint beauty aside, she wasn't going to stay here a moment longer. And now was as good a time as any to demand that Patrick MacDonald take her home.

***

Patrick nodded at what Brianna told him, not at all surprised.

"I know she's angry with me," he said. "But I had no choice."

Brianna threw up her hands, her blue eyes snapping. "I won't argue with you. Though I'm sure Tara won't be so accommodating."

Patrick laughed without humor. "Of that I have no doubt."

He stepped into the kitchen to find Tara standing there, her hands gripping the back of a chair. The expression on her face left little to the imagination. If she wasn't such a little thing, he'd almost expect her to lift the chair and crash it over his head.

"Tara," he said.

She opened her mouth to speak, stilling as she glanced at Bryce. With a tight smile, she faced him again. "I must speak with you, Patrick MacDonald."

"Aye, lass." He walked past her to the back door and opened it. "Come walk with me."

She let out a grunt of frustration and stomped in front of him into the morning sunshine. The light bounced off her shining locks, and her ponytail caught his eye as it swung back and forth with each angry step. Aye, his ears would be blistered for sure.

He closed the door and followed her to a bench set beneath one thick tree. She sat on the edge and faced him. When she opened her mouth again, he held up one hand to still her.

"I need your help, Tara."

She paused, then shook her head. "Look, Mr. MacDonald. I don't know what you think you need, but I'm not staying her another minute." She stood, shaking. "Take me home."

His shoulders slumped. "Ah, lass. I can't do that."

He saw she caught something in his tone. Her brow furrowed, she peered up at him. He let out a breath and sat down.

"What is it?" she asked, her voice clipped but steady.

She was amazing, this girl. Out of her world, out of her time, and still he sensed a strength about her.

He bade her to sit again and she did, obviously careful to keep from direct contact with him. He couldn't blame her for her fear. Hadn't he taken her from her home yesterday?

"It's my son, Tara." He placed his hands on his thighs. "He's wee, just three years old. He needs your help more than I."

"Your son?"

He saw it in her eyes, a flicker of the concern he'd seen so clearly yesterday. He would appeal to her love of children. To her desire to see them well and whole. His hands fisted, but he ignored a niggling of guilt at the back of his mind. There was no time for it, and if he had to use her sensitivities so be it.

"Aye. He came to live with me nearly a week ago. He's troubled, Tara. And I need you to see to him. To help him."

Her amber eyes grew round. "What's wrong with him?"

He opened his mouth and closed it after a moment. He couldn't tell her about the Banshee. Time travel was amazing enough to her. He feared that if he told her she was among Faery folk here in the dell she would do more than faint.

"Devlin's locked away in himself, Tara. I can't reach him. Luke's Pix— Brianna can't reach him even with her special talents. And the people here..." Tears of anger choked his throat and he banged his fists on his thighs. "They call him a changeling, Tara. A devil. But he's not!"

Tara touched his fisted hand, her fingers cool against his flesh. "I'm sorry about your son. But what can I do?"

He gazed into her eyes, seeing the concern, the urge to help, and knew once more he had chosen well.

"I need what you *know*, Tara. From your studies at the Children's Hospital. If you help him?" He swallowed. "If you can help bring him back to me, I'll take you home."

She blinked and pulled back from him, that wariness evident in her gaze once more. "You would keep me here against my will?"

There it was. He let out a breath and gave her a reluctant nod.

"Aye." When she pulled away and began to stand, he grasped her wrist. "But not for me, lass. For Devlin." Tara stared down at his hand and he released her. "I'm sorry. Pray, come see him. He needs help. And you're the only one who can give it to him."

Tara stood and turned from him, her arms crossed. Patrick held his breath while she gave his offer obvious thought. He wished he could know what she was thinking, who she was regretting leaving behind in Indianapolis, what life she thought to return to after helping him.

She spun on her heel, determination clear on her face, and he dared to hope she'd accept.

"All right, Patrick." She lifted her chin. "I'll see your son. But I'm not making any promises."

Patrick nearly wept with relief. He stood and grabbed her to him, holding her close. She felt so good in his arms, like a bundle of hope. "I'm grateful to you, lass. Aye, so grateful."

When she stiffened against him he realized their position. He released her as if she burned and raked his fingers through his hair. "Forgive me, Tara."

She waved her hand, but he didn't miss the pretty pink blush on her cheeks. He would try his hardest to ignore the warmth it spread through him.

"It's all right." She squared her shoulders. "I'll give you my answer after I see him. I don't know if I can help him, but I'll see him. Take me to your son, Patrick. Take me to Devlin."

Chapter 6

Tara walked beside Patrick, her mind racing. The pretty
views, the picturesque cottages, barely registered in her
mind as she worked through all Patrick had told her. And all
he hadn't.

She'd had no idea a child was involved. She'd suspect
the man of knowing her weakness if he hadn't waited until
this morning to tell her about the boy. Yes, her work was no
secret, but her reasons behind it were. Every child should
have a connection to their family. Wasn't that what drove
her own work?

What could be wrong with this child? Patrick said he
couldn't reach his son. Could the child be autistic? Mentally
disabled or diminished somehow?

She slanted a look at the big man walking briskly at her
left, and saw a jumble of expressions. Did Patrick realize he
wore a mixture of emotions on his face? She looked ahead.
Maybe only someone with Tara's background in human
behavior would see it, but the man was troubled with a
capital T.

She peeked at him from the corner of her eye. He
certainly looked different this morning in his loose shirt and

pants tucked into shining boots. Quite… dashing. And very different from the man who wore jeans and a flannel shirt yesterday. God, had it only been yesterday?

She glanced around at the quaint buildings in the charming but certainly primitive town. Perhaps Patrick's son was no more than deaf. Surely people in this time wouldn't be able to deal with a handicapped child, no matter how mild the impairment. When she imagined such cruelty or ignorance her heart gave a twist. Oh, to be shunned was a cruel fate no child should suffer.

The crushed stone of the road crunched beneath his boots as her sneakers silently kept pace. She longed to ask him more, but now his handsome face was shuttered.

"There's my family's workshop," Patrick said, finally breaking their quiet.

Tara looked at the long building, and at the cheery storefront with broad windows. What had Bryce told her? Shoes. The MacDonalds made shoes. Her gaze fell to Patrick's boots once more. Nice. And very pricy if they'd been bought at the mall in downtown Indianapolis. Again, she glanced at his clothes. They were obviously very fine, despite being outdated. She swallowed a slightly hysterical laugh. No, not outdated. She gave her head a shake. So the MacDonalds must do all right for themselves.

Made plenty of gold, or shillings or stinkin' doubloons, for all she knew.

As they passed several shops and homes, no one greeted Patrick with more than a curt nod, their eyes narrowed. Tara felt Patrick's anger in that moment, when those same people gazed at her with open distrust. These people treated a little boy like he was the devil? She longed to shout out that all children were blessings, even the troubled ones. But her jeans and T-shirt drew more attention than she wished, so she kept her mouth shut. An angry mob was something no one needed this morning.

Patrick turned down a tree-lined lane to the left and she followed. She soon saw a large buff-colored house with three thick peaked roofs. Smoke curled from one of the chimneys at the back of the house, most likely the kitchen. It was a pretty house and impressive in its way. Certainly in comparison to the modest cottages she'd seen on their short walk, and this seemed to confirm what she'd assumed about the MacDonalds' success. The hostility she'd sensed from the villagers seemed even more out of place, given the family's apparent standing.

When they stepped on the covered front porch, Patrick

at last stopped. He placed his hand on her arm and she looked up into his face. His concern was visible, but so was his uncertainty. Tara felt a tremor in her heart.

"Devlin was quiet this mornin', Tara," he said. "But I don't know how he'll be now."

She offered him a slight smile and gave his hand a pat. "It's all right. I want to see him."

Relief filled his eyes as it had back at Brianna's house. He released her arm and she sighed. Tara bit her tongue so she wouldn't voice her thoughts. She was no miracle worker, and this man seemed to think that she held some secret to his son's recovery. He pushed open the front door and waved her in ahead of him.

"Uncle?" he called, shutting the door behind them.

"Aye, Patrick," came a man's voice.

A man came into the room. He was an older gentleman, and dapperly dressed. His green eyes were both sharp and kind as they took her in.

He smiled and inclined his head. "Hello, Miss." He rounded on Patrick. "Is this the girl you took, you bloody fool?"

Tara knew the man's irritation wasn't focused on her. Patrick shifted on his big feet, looking like a little boy for a second.

"This is Tara Connor, Uncle. From Indianapolis." He turned to Tara. "Tara, this is my Uncle Seamus."

She held out her hand and Patrick's uncle took it and brought it to his lips. His eyes sparkled and she knew from where the MacDonalds got their lauded charm.

"'Tis a pleasure, Tara Connor. Pray don't let my nephew's foolish act lead you to believe all we MacDonalds are daft."

Brianna time traveled. Patrick used his charm on her, Tara was now in the year 1814? *Daft?* Crazy and out of her own mind maybe. The MacDonalds seemed as normal as anyone else here.

Tara smiled and shook her head. "I won't, sir." She once more saw the man fix a glare on Patrick and faced him herself. "Take me to your son, Patrick."

Patrick nodded and walked down a hallway, Tara following closely behind. At what must be a bedroom door, he once more faced her with both relief and concern etched on his face.

"Thank you, Tara. I know you can help him."

Tara wished she was as certain of that fact as Patrick

was. He opened the door and she looked past him into the room. The large carved bed was empty, except for rumpled linens. It took her a second to spot the child, who was curled into a ball in the corner. He was so tiny, she could hardly believe he was three years old.

"He used to sleep on the floor," Patrick said in a low voice.

Nesting, she guessed. That wasn't uncommon with kids suffering from emotional or mental conditions. Her heart tight, she stepped closer to the boy. He shifted onto his bottom, hugging his knees to his chest as he stared ahead.

He was such a beautiful child, with curls the same strawberry blond as his father. Thick black lashes framed vacant blue eyes. His pale cheeks were porcelain smooth and his little mouth, which if animated would probably be a perfect cupid's bow, was slack.

"Devlin," Patrick said, crouching down beside his son. "This is Tara Connor. She's going to help you, son."

The boy gave no indication he'd heard his father, and Patrick didn't say more. His shoulders were set and stiff, as if he longed to touch the boy but didn't dare.

Tara chose to take Patrick's continued silence as her cue. "Hello, Devlin," she began. She settled beside him on the floor, wrapping her arms around her knees to replicate his posture and to make herself smaller. "I came from far away to meet you. I've heard a lot about you."

She sensed the child heard her, for his long lashes flickered as he nearly blinked. She slowly reached toward him, her gaze focused for any reaction. She touched his arm and he flinched, squeezing his eyes shut. But he didn't move away.

She withdrew her hand. "Devlin, I know we just met. But I'd like to play with you some time. I bet we could be friends. Would you like that?"

The boy flicked his gaze at her, his large blue eyes showing nearly nothing. Her heart twisted again. The next instant he began to rock, pulling from her as he stared at the floor. She took one glance at Patrick and her heart nearly broke. The anguish on his face cut into her. She looked at Devlin and forced a smile.

"I'll be back to see you later, Devlin," she said in a bright voice.

The boy stilled for a moment, then continued his rocking.

Tara walked to the door, turning when she realized

Patrick didn't follow. She saw him ruffle the boy's curls before dropping a kiss on his head. The man loved his son. That was crystal clear. Her throat tight, she stepped into the hall to wait for him.

"Mrs. O'Grady will look after him," he said as he joined her. "Can you help him, Tara? Lass, I pray you can help him."

Could she? Tara didn't believe the boy was deaf, so that left any number of possible afflictions causing his condition. But with her training she would try. She couldn't leave here without trying to reach Devlin, to attempt to bring him back to his father. And she knew Patrick's ultimatum wasn't the reason. Any child who had a chance to make a connection with his family should take it. Tara would see to it.

"I'll try my best, Patrick."

He reached for her and she thought he would hug her as he had at Brianna's house. But he dropped his hands and reddened. She felt her cheeks heat and looked away.

"I'll go borrow some of Brianna's things for you, Tara." He rubbed the back of his neck. "That is, will you be stayin' here with Devlin?"

Tara thought for a moment. She couldn't stay at Brianna's house. She had a husband and toddler to care for. And Tara

95

knew Patrick's uncle lived in this house, so there wouldn't be any impropriety. *Impropriety?* Oh, she was beginning to think like a nineteenth century woman!

"Yes. I'll stay."

Patrick gave a curt nod. He showed her to a room down the hall from his. As lovely as the room she was in last night, this one was opulent. It was decorated with fine cherry furniture that would make an antique dealer sigh. She walked into the room and sat on the bed, bouncing a bit.

He paused in the doorway, as if reluctant to cross the threshold. "There's a water closet down the hall."

She gave him a small smile. "Brianna?"

Patrick returned the expression. "Aye."

With that, he closed the door and left her to her thoughts. Tara crossed to a small desk set against one wall and pulled open a drawer. She withdrew several pieces of paper and sat in the chair. To her surprise she discovered a pen made of plastic in the drawer. She rolled it in her fingers, and the plastic felt smooth and familiar beneath her touch. It was imprinted with bright blue letters and a horseshoe: *Indianapolis Colts*. She chuckled and pulled off the pen cap.

First, she would write her observations from her short visit with Devlin. Then she would make a list of the milestones and their indicators, hoping to gauge the boy's development—or lack of it. As she neared the end of the list, her spirits were low.

Even from her brief visit with the child, she knew he was quite troubled. There was so much to accomplish here in this time. She glanced at her watch, surprised to see it was still running. Time was surely relative. Wasn't it only yesterday she was at the behavior lab?

Her mind went to her little apartment in Indianapolis, a city that didn't even exist yet. She rubbed her forehead. Well, she doubted anyone there would miss her. She had no one in the city, not even a close friend. Studying to satisfy her grants and scholarships had left little time for socializing. And until she sat here in this lovely room in the past, she hadn't really given much thought to the state of her life.

Mark had called her cold, unable to let anyone close. His parting words still stung, though more than a year had passed since the disaster that had been her one close relationship ended. Maybe he was right.

A knock came at the door and she started. She eyed the wood panel, wondering if Patrick had returned.

"Yes?"

The door opened and a round gray-haired old lady peeped inside. "Hello, dear." A smile showed on her face. "I'm Mrs. O'Grady.

This must be the housekeeper Patrick had mentioned. Tara stood, brushed her hands over her thighs and extended her hand.

"It's very nice to meet you, Mrs. O'Grady."

The lady's brows shot upward as she shook her head and bobbed a curtsey. Whoops. Tara dropped her hand to her side.

"I fixed a bit o' somethin' for you to eat," the woman said. "Master Patrick says you'll be stayin' here to help the little mite, and I'm to get ya' settled."

"I... Yes. Thank you."

The lady smiled and bobbed another curtsey. She spun on her heel and waved a hand in the air so Tara followed.

"The water closet be down that hall," Mrs. O'Grady said as she walked toward the living area. "I put some o' Miss Brianna's things in there she said ya' kin use. I'll see to the dresses and such when Master Patrick brings 'em."

"Thank you, Mrs. O'Grady." She followed the woman

into the dining room, a pretty room with a long table of dark wood and a matching sideboard. On the sideboard was a tempting spread of salads and bread and cheese. Her stomach rumbled and she crossed to the buffet. "This all looks so wonderful."

"Help yourself, dear." She turned to leave the room. "I'll be in the kitchen if ya' need anything."

Tara nodded. As she served herself some ham salad, she heard tuneful whistling from outside. It grew louder until the front door opened. Tara glanced through the archway to find Patrick's uncle smiling in her direction.

"Hello, Tara lass." He rubbed his hands together and joined her at the sideboard. "Ah, Mrs. O'Grady sets a fine luncheon, she does."

Tara nodded her agreement and sat at the table. Patrick's uncle wore his fine clothes well, and she'd bet that as a young man he would have come close to rivaling Patrick in the looks department. Tara shook her head. She'd never been so focused on a man's... attributes before seeing Patrick's handsome face yesterday.

She glanced down at her own drab clothes, feeling out of place in her jeans and T-shirt. Maybe wearing some of Brianna's things wouldn't be so terrible.

"What's your thinkin' on the boy, Tara?" Seamus asked after a short while.

Tara wiped her mouth with a fine linen napkin and then folded it once more. "I'll need to spend more time with him," she said. "But I can think of several things I might try." She glanced around the pretty dining room, her mind working. "Does Devlin eat here with the family?"

"Nay," Seamus answered, his brows drawn together. "Why?"

"I think it would help him begin to relate to all of you if he shared your meals. And he has to learn to connect with the people around him."

Seamus's green eyes were thoughtful as he stroked his dimpled chin. "Aye, a connection."

"The child eatin' here, Miss Tara?" Mrs. O'Grady asked. She set a tray of fragrant cookies on the table and straightened. "But he barely eats when I feed him in Master Patrick's room."

Tara knew these people were trying to deal with Devlin's problems as best they could, and didn't want to push them. But the child needed to feel a connection to his family, and meal time would be a good place to start.

"We'll give dinner a try tonight, Mrs. O'Grady." Tara faced Seamus. "That is, if you have no objections?"

"Nay," Patrick's uncle said with a shake of his red head. "If you think it would help him, lass, then he'll eat here with his family."

Tara's shoulders relaxed. "Good." The aroma of the cookies reached her, lemony and sweet. "Oh, Mrs. O'Grady! Those cookies smell wonderful."

"Cookies? Oh, ya' mean the biscuits."

Tara smiled. "Yes. May I take some to Devlin?"

Mrs. O'Grady sniffled as she bobbed her head. "Oh, I made 'em for the little mite." She dabbed one eye with the corner of her apron. "Thought as they be the MacDonald lads' favorites all these years he might favor them too."

Tara took a few cookies and placed them in another napkin, flashing a smile at the older woman. "I bet he'll like them, then. After he wakes up I'll give him some of your delicious biscuits."

The housekeeper gave Tara a watery smile and hurried into the kitchen. Seamus winked at Tara and they went back to their meal.

After lunch, Tara looked in on Devlin. He slept on a little

bed against one wall, though kicking and twitching was no way to get any true rest. She tiptoed to the bed and sat on the edge, reaching out to gently stroke his red-gold curls. She studied his fair skin, which was flawless and smooth. His rosy lips were turned down in a pout.

He was a beautiful child, with an otherworldly look to him. That thought gave Tara a start and she withdrew her hand. Patrick was able to bring her here from her own time. And Brianna traveled back and forth to the future on shopping sprees. She couldn't imagine how they came to have toilets and running water here, either. No! If she ignored the fact that she was in Ireland in the year 1814, everything here was as normal as back home. The MacDonalds were nothing more than normal good-looking people who could time travel.

She smoothed her finger over the boy's cheek and left him to his troubled nap.

Chapter 7

Tara peeked into the bathroom in the hall. What the heck?
She gave in to the temptation and took a shower in the well-
appointed "water closet." Hot water. She wasn't surprised.
Though the thick bar of soap wasn't the bath gel she was used to,
she found it lathered well and left her skin and hair soft. She
dried herself with a thick towel and wrapped herself with it. She
picked up her discarded clothes and hurried to her room.

She noticed a comb and brush set on the vanity then, and
some hair pins and ribbons. She picked up the comb and worked
it through her curls. A glance at the open doors of the carved
armoire showed her several dresses hanging there. Curious, she
set down the comb and walked to the wardrobe. The dresses
were light and soft, and made of cotton or muslin in pale colors
with little cap sleeves. She touched the one nearest her, a white
dress dotted with little yellow roses. Cotton slips hung beside the
dresses, and on the shelf above were what looked like baggy
underwear and tights. No corset? Nice.

"I love the nineteenth century," she said to herself.

She pulled on the tights, they were really like thick silk
socks, and underwear. She eyed the scooped necklines of the
dresses. "Hmm, no bra." She put on one of the slips, adjusting

the thin straps at her shoulders.

She chose the white and yellow dress and stood in front of the long mirror in the corner. "Not bad."

She tied the thin yellow ribbon beneath her breasts and stepped into soft leather slippers. "And these must be a pair of 'fine MacDonald shoes,'" She held out one foot. "Very pretty and quite comfortable."

Clueless about what to do with her hair, she simply pulled it back and tied it with a white ribbon from the vanity. She grabbed the wrapped cookies for Devlin and left the room.

"Oh, Miss Tara!" Mrs. O'Grady said in the hall. "Ya' be a pretty picture."

Tara waved away the compliment. "Thank you for arranging the dresses and things, Mrs. O'Grady. Is Devlin awake?"

"Aye, miss."

She nodded her thanks and went to Patrick's room, gathering all of her knowledge and strength around her as she always did in preparation for her work in the behavioral lab.

She found Devlin on the floor, once again with his

skinny arms wrapped around his knees. He appeared calm, but she knew what torment could be going on inside his little body.

"Hello, Devlin," she said with a bright smile. "Mrs. O'Grady told me you had a nice nap."

Devlin didn't say anything in response, though he did lift his head a fraction. She took that as a sign of encouragement and joined him on the floor, tucking her skirt beneath her folded legs.

"Mrs. O'Grady makes the yummiest cook— biscuits, Devlin." She unwrapped the sweet treasures and held them in front of him. "Have you tasted one today?"

A flicker of his lashes showed he eyed the treats. Tara brought one to her mouth and took a bite, tasting lemon and honey and sunshine. These were the perfect cookies for a little boy wrapped in darkness.

"Mmm," she said with exaggeration. "Yummy."

Devlin eyed the cookies in the napkin. She wanted him to take a one from her hand, but didn't dare hope that would happen right away. She placed the open napkin on the floor at his feet instead, leaving the two cookies to tempt him. One little hand shot out and he grabbed one, bringing it to his mouth. He chewed with his mouth open, devouring the cookie. He was so little, and obviously hungry. She wondered if he ever had enough to eat before Patrick brought him here.

"It's good, isn't it?" she asked.

One often-used technique was to state the child's feelings as if he was saying them. And the delight on his little face made that task easy today. He licked his lips and reached for the other cookie. In a flash it too was gone.

"Oh, you like Mrs. O'Grady's biscuits!" Tara said, clapping her hands together. "She'll be so pleased."

Devlin was still again, but his body tensed as he paid attention to her. Tara took the empty napkin and wiped the crumbs from his face. He flinched slightly.

"You don't like getting your face cleaned," she said. "But you're so handsome, Devlin. You look just like your papa."

At the mention of Patrick the boy lifted his head and looked toward the door. Tara knew this was a good sign. That he anticipated Patrick's return.

"Your papa's at the workshop, Devlin. He's making shoes." She touched the toe of one of his sturdy little boots. "I bet he made these."

Devlin still looked at the door. She thought she'd try another technique, and mirrored his actions. She sat closer to him, facing the door.

"Your papa will be back to see you soon, Devlin," she said. "He loves you very much."

He faced her and she caught a flicker of something in his eyes, an odd glimmer she'd never seen in the autistic children in her care in Indianapolis. It caused her skin to dimple in goose bumps. Devlin was locked in there, but she knew in her heart that he wanted to come out.

"I thought you could eat with us at the big table tonight, Devlin," she went on. "Won't that be nice?"

She edged closer to him and he scooted away a fraction.

"Oh, I'll get your spot!" she said cheerfully. "You can't have all the good sitting space."

Using another technique she'd used in the past, she followed him. As he continued to pull away, she laughed as if it was a grand game they played. At last he was in the corner and she thought she saw his mouth lift slightly. She felt a surge of encouragement.

Before she could risk crowding him, she pulled back. She stood and crossed to the window. "It's a lovely day outside. Have you looked outside today, Devlin?"

The little boy was still now, but his head tilted toward her.

Tara looked at her watch, surprised to see that nearly half an hour had passed. The child was a draw to her, but she didn't want to press him. Twenty to thirty minutes of "floor time," as it was called, was really the limit. But she could observe him for a while yet.

She turned to him, her hands clasped. "I'll bring some toys for you, Devlin. I bet your papa has some toys for you." He faced her then, and she knew it was a direct response to her mention of Patrick again. That man was the key to the boy's recovery, and the one who could do more than she could alone. And Patrick didn't even know it.

"I'll ask your papa when he comes home," she said. "Then we can play."

She stepped closer to Devlin. Unable to resist, she touched the boy's curls. He didn't pull away, but he didn't respond either.

"I'll be back in a little while, Devlin," she said.

She returned to her room and picked up her notes. Mentally exhausted, but much more encouraged than she had been at their initial session, she settled at the desk. The child wanted to make a connection. She'd felt it. Once more she thought of that flash or glimmer in his eyes. Something wasn't quite right, though.

She recalled her impression as the boy slept, that he seemed different. She couldn't put into words what she suspected, and wouldn't burden Patrick with such foolishness. Devlin was troubled, and that had to be her focus. Grabbing up her notes and the Colts pen, she returned to Devlin's room.

She perched on the edge of the neatly-made bed and watched the child as he played with the laces on his shoes. The shadow of an expression, a wistfulness, crossed his face. Did he think about his father? She wrote down her impressions and settled in to keep an eye on the boy.

She took few notes, as he didn't do much for a long while. Her gaze strayed to the window, taking in the lovely day visible outside. A bird call, loud and jarring, suddenly broke her trance. Devlin screamed, running toward the nearest corner as if he wanted to bury himself in it. He began to pound his hands against the wall, clawing at the plaster as he tried to hide himself.

"Devlin!" Tara cried.

She ran to him and grabbed his hands. He grunted as he fought her. He was stronger than his size should indicate. But she held on tightly, whispering soothing words as she stilled his flailing arms.

"It's all right, Devlin," she said, wrapping him in her arms. "The loud bird scared you," she stated. "You want to hide from the bird. But the bird can't get you."

He began to shake and she felt it clear to her soul. He cuddled against her, curled into himself rather than embracing her. She held him to her breast, rocking back and forth as his body lost its rigidity. Finally, his slack body collapsed against her and she brushed his damp curls away from his brow.

"There," she said, her eyes stinging. "You feel better now. Relaxed. I'm glad."

She held him like that as long as he would allow. Soon he scrambled off her lap to stand against the wall. She wanted to hold him again, but wouldn't push him. Not now.

"You want your space," she said with a nod. "I'll sit on the bed again."

She did as she said, still watching him as he sank back down to the floor. But his gaze slid to her now and then, and it was enough to give her what she so wanted to give his father. Hope.

***

110

"She's stayin' with us?" Sean asked Patrick as they walked home.

"Aye, Sean. She needs to attend to Devlin."

Sean nodded. "What does she look like?"

Patrick stilled. He wouldn't tell his brother that Tara was the prettiest girl he'd ever seen. Or that when he'd held her that afternoon he wanted to never let her go. Sean would think him daft for sure.

"She's very fair," he offered.

Sean turned sharply, narrowing his eyes. "You favor the girl?"

"Nay!" Patrick snapped. He raked his fingers through his hair. "I don't need a woman, Sean. Not after the Banshee. But, Devlin... Devlin needs her."

It was Sean's turn to shrug and Patrick sighed. He resumed walking. 'Twas a pity he didn't believe the subject dropped. At least the pup hadn't ask Patrick to describe the lass. He knew he wouldn't be able to disguise the fact that he found her very much to his liking.

Tara was quite pretty. With all that sable hair and those big amber eyes. And her future clothes hid little of her fetching figure from him.

That morning, as the girl spoke to Devlin, he'd known he'd done the right thing. She was the one to pull Devlin from his suffering. But Patrick was torn between wanting desperately to check on Tara's progress and wanting to shield himself from her possible failure. Lord, he would give anything for Devlin. He prayed that Tara would be enough.

"I'd cease that scowlin', brother," Sean teased as they stepped onto the front porch. "You'll scare the girl right back to the future."

Patrick bit back a retort and entered the house. The sight that met him was surprising. Uncle Seamus sat in his place at the head of the table, with Tara to his right. And there, in the chair beside her, was Devlin. His head was down, his gaze fixed on the table linen, but he was there.

"Good evening," Patrick said, stepping toward the dining room.

As he did so, his eyes shifted to Tara. She wore one of Brianna's dresses. To advantage, in his considered opinion. She was so lovely.

"Hello, Tara," Sean said, coming forward to sketch a bow. "I'm Sean MacDonald."

Tara nodded her head, a smile on her face. "Hello, Sean. It's a pleasure to meet you."

Patrick frowned at his brother, whose green eyes were dancing with mirth. And interest, damn it.

"Uncle," Patrick said. "Tara." He stepped closer and saw that Devlin was perched on several books. "Hello, Devlin."

The little boy lifted his head to stare at him. Patrick nearly lost his breath. Devlin's eyes were crystal clear and, for that brief moment, Patrick believed his son actually saw him. Devlin soon lowered his head and grabbed up the roll Tara placed in front of him.

"You like the bread, Devlin," she stated.

The boy said nothing. Uncle Seamus and Sean exchanged a look of confusion, but from what little Patrick knew of Tara he knew she didn't do anything without a purpose. He caught her eye and she offered him a smile of encouragement.

"You're hungry, son," he offered as Devlin took another bite of the roll.

Tara's gorgeous smile was worth the small effort. He smiled in response, feeling a bit like a daft boy. He turned to find Sean gazing at the girl in rapture. Bloody hell.

"Come, Sean," he said, shoving him with his shoulder. "We

need to wash for dinner."

At last his brother pulled his gaze from Tara. Patrick would need to keep an eye on him. The pup was as blessed with the MacDonald charm as the rest of them.

When Patrick rejoined the family at the table, he sat at the end opposite Seamus. From there he watched Tara speak to, and for, Devlin as the boy devoured the savory stew. It was one of Mrs. O'Grady's specialties, and though Devlin wore most of it on his little face it was clear that he liked the stuff as much as his father did.

Tara ate gracefully, as he'd suspected she would. By her dress and demeanor, anyone in the dell would think her born and raised in this time. But he knew the strong woman within the pleasing form, and she wouldn't be Tara without that strength.

"Were you lads busy this day, Patrick?" Uncle Seamus asked.

"Aye," he said.

"Winter was tough on shoes," Sean put in. "And we're all too pleased to sell replacements."

Seamus laughed as he nodded his agreement and Patrick caught that smile on Tara's lips again. The sight warmed his belly. Forcing his attention to his meal, he took a large bite of bread and chewed.

The meal was pleasant with the addition of the two newcomers to the table, and Patrick watched Devlin and Tara closely. She was patient with the boy, speaking softly yet clearly as she righted his spilled bowl or wiped his face.

"I got sweets fer ya', lads," Mrs. O'Grady said at the end of the meal.

"Oh, Devlin!" Tara said as the boy raised his head. "You like sweets. And Mrs. O'Grady made them, like the biscuits you ate today."

Patrick glanced at his son. The housekeeper had only been able to get him to eat broth, and only by feeding him herself. Tara gave the boy some independence as she directed his meal. Again, he knew she was the one to help him. He thought of his promise to take her home once Devlin was well. 'Twas only right. He ignored the faint gnawing sensation in his belly.

Devlin ate three biscuits, loudly and with obvious delight. The expression of pleasure on his little face warmed Patrick himself, brief though it was. Devlin soon began to shift in his chair, and his gaze darted about the room.

"I'll take the little mite to the water closet, Miss Tara," Mrs.

115

O'Grady said.

Tara thanked her and watched as the child let the housekeeper lead him to the bathroom. Patrick saw the worry on her face. And the hope.

"Well, now," Uncle Seamus began, coming to his feet. "I have a bit o' readin' awaitin' me in the study."

He shot a look of meaning in Sean's direction, and Patrick hid his smile. Sean shot to his feet and bowed again.

"Miss Tara," he said. He turned to Patrick. "Brother."

He left the dining room and Tara began to rise.

"Pray sit, Tara," Patrick said.

***

Tara watched as Patrick rose and sat down in his uncle's chair. He folded his hands and placed them on the table. They were strong-looking, capable hands.

"That was amazing," he said.

She felt a blush creep up her cheeks. She would focus on his words, and not on the clean fresh scent of him as he leaned closer. "Devlin needs to feel connected, Patrick. Mealtime is a wonderful opportunity for that."

His blue eyes were round as he stared at her. "But he looked at me, Tara. When I spoke to him, he looked right at me."

She nodded, pleased that he saw the importance in that brief connection.

"I've seen these flashes of awareness a few times today." She thought to ask him more pointed questions about his son. "Did you spend time with Devlin before he came to live here?"

His brow furrowed. "Nay."

She blinked. Why didn't Patrick see his son before now? And who was Devlin's mother?

"And yet he feels a connection to you," she stated.

"Do you really think so?"

The desperation was clear on his face and Tara refrained from hugging him as she had Devlin. She doubted she would feel the least bit maternal with the big man pressed against her.

"Yes," she said. "I made a point to mention you to him, and I got some response."

"Ah." The wistfulness in his voice touched her. "It's what I pray for," he murmured.

Her heart skipped a beat and she eased her chair away from him.

"I'd like to review my notes with you," she said.

He shook his head. "I know nothing of your work, lass. I

trust you in this."

"But, don't you want to know?"

He held up one hand and came to his feet. "You're the one to help him, Tara. It's my duty to keep him warm and safe. And I shall."

"But you should play a part in his therapy, Patrick. You can help him."

Sadness filled his eyes before he tore his gaze from hers. He gave a slow shake of his head.

"Nay," he rasped. "I'm the one who did this to him."

Chapter 8

Tara was struck speechless. Many of the parents she'd encountered went through a period when they questioned every little thing they'd done during the pregnancy or following the birth, all to finally come to the conclusion that Autism often had no single cause. But Patrick's conviction was so strong she didn't dare argue with him. Not now.

"I'll keep working with him," she said. "And you're welcome to join us whenever you're able."

He gave another shake of his head. Tara stood and placed her hand on his arm. Patrick grew rigid as his gaze met hers again. Her belly gave a flutter as she stared up at him. He was in so much pain. Almost as much as Devlin.

"Tara," he whispered.

Her name on his lips sent a shiver through her. She remembered the moment—was it only that morning?—when he had held her. In gratitude, yes, but she was afraid to think of the sensation he'd cause her should he hold her for a different purpose. With his blue eyes so compelling and his body so close to hers.

Mrs. O'Grady entered the room and Tara stepped away from Patrick.

"The mite be in Master Patrick's room, Miss Tara," she said.

Tara lowered her gaze and brushed her hands over her skirt.

"All… all right, Mrs. O'Grady," she said. "Thank you."

She turned to Patrick. "Would you like to come with me?"

He opened his mouth, finally letting out a breath. "Nay, lass. You see to the boy."

She couldn't force him. She'd have to find a way to bring him into Devlin's therapy. She was certain he was the key to the child's recovery. And perhaps the child was the key to Patrick's happiness as well.

She gave him a nod and joined Devlin in the bedroom. The child sat on the floor once again.

"Do you want to sit on your bed, Devlin?" she asked brightly. She perched on his bed. "Oh, it's nice and so soft."

He turned his head to just catch her eye. She had seen that expression on his father's face just moments ago. Desire and reluctance.

She leaned toward him and held out her hand. His arm nearest her twitched and he froze, clenching his hand into a fist. Taking a different approach, she moved over on the bed and leaned back on her elbows.

"Would you like to hear a story, Devlin?" she asked. She looked around the room. "I don't see any books, but I bet we can borrow some tomorrow from your cousin, Bryce. Bryce is as old as you are, Devlin."

He watched her closely. But still he held back.

"I want to tell you some stories," she said with a nod. "I hope you'll like them."

She began to tell him of a mermaid who wished to be human, of a girl who lived with seven dwarves, of a princess sleeping for many years until her prince kissed her awake. Thank God for her good memory. She'd gone to see the animated movies by herself over the past decade or so, and hoped the tales gave Devlin as much pleasure now as they had her then.

Devlin's lids began to droop and she took advantage of his fatigue.

"Come, Devlin," she said softly, coming to her feet. "You can rest here beside me."

She scooped him up in her arms and he didn't fight her. He didn't relax, though. He was very stiff.

After placing him on his bed, she removed his shoes. He

121

grunted his protest until she placed the shoes next to his pillow beside his head. He faced the shoes, his sleepy eyes focused nonetheless.

She told him another story, one of a girl who fell asleep in the future and woke up in the past. The sound of her voice lulled him into fitful sleep and she couldn't resist brushing his curls back from his face.

"Good night, Devlin," she whispered.

She eased off the bed and stretched. She walked softly to the door and when she pulled it open she found Patrick standing there. He filled the doorway, leaning one arm on the doorjamb. His hair was damp, like he'd just washed his face. The collar of his shirt was opened and she stared at his strong throat. His spicy fresh scent was stronger with him so close to her, and she couldn't resist sucking in a breath of him.

"Pardon me, lass," he rushed out.

She recovered her wits and cocked her head to one side. "Devlin's asleep, Patrick."

He nodded and she moved aside to let him in the room. He brushed against her as he did so, and she nearly went weak in the knees. Oh, she must be more tired than she thought. She ducked out into the hallway.

"Good night," she whispered.

She didn't wait for his response as she hurried to her bedroom.

***

Patrick watched Tara make good her escape. She hadn't known he'd stood outside the door for close to an hour before her discovery. Drawn to the room, he had stood and listened to the tales she told the child. Patrick closed the door and stepped toward the pallet.

Devlin slept uneasily. He didn't toss and turn, but his limbs weren't still. He dropped a kiss on Devlin's head and began to ready for bed.

"You liked Tara's storytellin', Devlin," he said softly.

He smiled to himself. He'd liked it, too. Her voice was as smooth as fine leather. Aye, but warm.

Stripped down to his breeches, he stretched out on his bed. He sniffed the air and could still detect Tara's scent in the room, flowers and freshness and woman. Thankfully she hadn't sat on his bed. Trying to sleep with her crowding his senses would surely prove torture.

As he had listened to her tell her tales to Devlin, his heart

123

had begun to ache. So long ago his mother would sit on his bed as she told him and his brothers tales of far off places and of funny happenings right there in the dell. And though Uncle Seamus had raised the brothers well after their parents died, Patrick always missed having a mother. A gentle soul who wanted nothing more than the happiness of her children and family.

Tara was much like his mother had been. Strong and sweet, good and pure. The stirring of desire struck his body and his heart. He squeezed his eyes shut and prayed for sleep.

Again the nightmare came, this time aided by his desire for the woman sleeping down the hall. In his sleeping mind Patrick stumbled through the woods, his arousal almost painful as the witch called to him.

"Aye, you want me," the Banshee purred. With a flick of her fingers she opened his breeches and stroked him, long and slow. "You ache to be inside me."

Patrick groaned, fisting his hands at his sides. The Banshee dropped to her knees in front of him, turning a sly smile upward. She took him in her mouth then, teasing and sucking until he nearly spent himself against her tongue.

She lifted her head away from him. "Nay, Patrick," she cooed, holding tight to his shaft. "I'll not let you spill your seed." She ran the tip of her tongue over the head and he gasped. "Not yet."

He fell to his own knees, leaning back on his heels as she crept over him. She straddled him, coming down hard to impale herself on his shaft as she pumped up and down. Patrick closed his eyes and leaned his head back, letting the witch take him with her over the edge to insanity.

In his lonely bed in the dell, Patrick twitched and moaned. He woke with a start, his heart pounding. His body was still erect, painful in his breeches as he tried to cool his ardor. Damn the Banshee and what she'd done to him. A whimper reached his ears and he turned to watch Devlin stirring in his sleep. That cooled his body at last.

Again he smelled it, the sweet scent of Tara.

"Please help Devlin, Tara," Patrick rasped.

He leaned back on his damp pillow and held a hand over his eyes. He wouldn't dare hope there was any help for himself.

***

Tara chose some lovely biscuits from the sideboard and sat at the beautiful dining table. The coffee in the carafe Mrs.

O'Grady had set on the table smelled heavenly and Tara poured some into a cup. A few teaspoons of sugar, and dollop of rich cream, and it was as good as anything from the coffee shop near the hospital. As she sniffed the aroma, her eyes closed, she could almost imagine herself home. Her eyes snapped open and she clicked her tongue. But she wasn't home.

Today she wore another of Brianna's borrowed dresses, this one in a pretty shade of blue. As strange as it was to wear such clothes, she found them comfortable. And last night she'd slept in one of her borrowed soft cotton slips, having no nightgown. It was all still so surreal, living here in the past.

The carved bed wasn't only beautiful but quite comfortable. She'd cracked the window a bit, letting in the freshest air she'd ever breathed. Yes, sleep had come easy, once she'd gotten Patrick out of her mind.

She'd tried to think of a way to reach him, of how he could help Devlin's treatment. It was so obvious the little boy needed him. At least he let Mrs. O'Grady dress and clean him, another indicator that Devlin wasn't completely closed off to the people around him. Again, she puzzled over the odd affliction holding on to him. Maybe Patrick wasn't being completely candid about Devlin's birth.

"Tara," a deep voice said softly.

She looked up to find Patrick standing in the doorway, his hair tousled and his brows drawn together. His blue eyes were dark and intense as they ran over her face, and she felt her skin prickle.

"Good morning," she answered. "I'd thought you would have left for your workshop."

He said something under his breath and shook his head. "Sean and Luke can open up this morning. I didn't sleep easy last night."

Suddenly an image popped into her mind, one of the big man tossing and turning, those thick lashes dark against his ruddy cheeks, that lovely mouth open as he moaned in his sleep. What did he wear to bed? She let out a slow breath. Did he sleep naked?

"Lass?" he asked, stepping closer to the table.

Tara wiped her damp palms on her linen napkin. God, since when was she such a pervert? She glanced over at him again. He licked his lips and she wanted to pressed her mouth there. Maybe this time-jump thing affected her in ways she couldn't imagine.

"Mrs. O'Grady is taking care of Devlin," she rushed out. "Getting him dressed and cleaned up. He'll be out to eat with us any minute."

He threw a troubled gaze toward the hallway, toward the bathroom, and shook his head again. "I'll leave you to his care, Tara."

She set aside any thought of how yummy he looked standing there, how well the clothes from the past—the now, really—fit his big body. "You have to take a role in his therapy. I feel it's crucial."

He opened his mouth, then bowed his head. "Good day, Tara."

He turned and left, leaving her speechless. Was it so painful for him to be around the son of the woman he'd lost? Jealousy cut through her and she drowned it with a deep drink of Mrs. O'Grady's strong coffee.

***

Patrick couldn't leave the cottage fast enough. First to find Tara, looking more beautiful in her borrowed finery than any woman had a right to, and then all but pleading with him to stay. Aye, he'd wanted to. He'd wanted to sit beside her at the table as if it was the most natural thing in the world. He'd wanted to take her small, capable hand in his and thank her for helping him. He'd wanted to lick the tiny biscuit crumb poised at the corner of her mouth.

His blood had pounded, it pounded still, and he couldn't pass it off as a lingering effect of last night's dream. Nay, 'twas Tara herself that caused his blood to run hot, not the memory of his wickedness with the Banshee.

Aye, he had wanted to stay with her. But the mention of poor Devlin set any thoughts of that aside. He couldn't bear to see the boy he'd cursed, not after last night. Not after a dream so clear it was as if his sin was fresh. As if his scar was raw. All his fault. He'd told Tara as much, though she'd obviously discounted what he'd said. No doubt many of the parents she'd spoken with in Indianapolis had said the same thing, had taken all the blame for their children's affliction on themselves. He let out a harsh laugh.

'Twas a pity he knew he was right.

Chapter 9

Tara would start Devlin's therapy right after breakfast, as she had each day for the past week. And as she'd found each morning of this past week, Patrick was nowhere to be found. Devlin ate at the table as if it was the norm for him, this time enjoying one of Mrs. O'Grady's sweet rolls. Sticky icing smeared his mouth and Tara smiled as she wiped his face with a napkin.

"You like that sweet roll, Devlin," she said.

Devlin said nothing but he didn't pull away from her. She took that as another small dose of encouragement. How much would Devlin respond if it was his father caring for him this morning?

Patrick MacDonald. She'd never met such a complicated man, and that wasn't even taking into account that he'd grabbed her from her time and whisked her to his. There was something there, something as dark as what she sometimes glimpsed in sweet Devlin's eyes. She drank her fragrant tea and pondered the man. And how she could help him get over whatever made his face go all dark and Gothic.

She'd graduated with honors, had studied at one of the leading centers for behavioral studies, and she couldn't reach the father one fraction of how she'd begun to reach the son. Again, she supposed he'd loved Devlin's mother very much to mourn her loss so. He never spoke of her, nor put any useless blame on her for Devlin's problems. No, he'd rather take them on himself. Oh, to be loved by such a man.

She set her pretty china tea cup down so quickly it clattered. Devlin had heard, she'd seen him flinch, but he was quiet for now. *Don't be stupid, Tara.*

It wouldn't do her any good to think of Patrick romantically. That was for sure. She never had much luck with her love life. The MacDonalds were a handsome bunch, though. She looked at the little boy in her temporary care. Surely little Devlin would easily draw the girls to him once he reached his teens.

She smiled as she once more sipped at her tea. She could imagine Devlin as a teen, laughing and teasing and completely at ease. Had Patrick been like that at one time? Had he been a charming boyfriend to Devlin's mother? Jealousy niggled at her, jealousy for the woman who had no part in the boy's life but had been such a big part of the father's.

Devlin began to chant, nonsense words to her ears. But aside from grunts or screams, she'd never heard him make any sounds. He babbled to his cup of milk and she saw he focused on a drop

131

of condensation on the glass. His eyes were clear at the moment and he seemed in control of his movements. Her heart lifted and any thought of romancing Patrick fled her mind. Devlin was ready for more challenges.

They played well together with Bryce's borrowed blocks and wooden animals, but her floor time with him could use the addition of some props. She reviewed the therapies in her mind. Maybe some dolls? She'd have to speak to Patrick about this.

"Good mornin', lass." Seamus greeted her with a grin. "And how's our little laddie?"

Devlin shrunk into himself but his eyes darted toward his great uncle. Tara hid her smile at the man's unusual attire. The green he sported today was bright, and with his red hair and brawny stature he looked almost like a— No, she thought in the next moment. They were in Ireland, yes. Seamus was as charming as the other MacDonalds. But Seamus *wasn't* a Leprechaun.

"Devlin's enjoying his pastry," she said.

Seamus nodded and served himself from the sideboard. "And what are you doin' this day, lass?"

"We'll play outside today, I think. And read some

books." Tara saw that Devlin hung on Seamus's every motion. "Devlin likes stories."

"Aye," Seamus chuckled. He sat down across from her and Devlin. "Like his father before him. 'Tis true sometimes the only way I could get the lads to be still was to tell them tales."

"You spent a lot of time with them, then?" she asked.

"Aye, lass. I raised 'em, I did." His mouth turned down in a slight frown. "Their parents died when the lads were wee things."

Tara nodded, thoughtful. "And Patrick and Sean still live with you," she said.

"Aye. Sean's too young to worry about settlin' down into his own place. And Patrick—"

Seamus stopped himself, his gaze sliding away from hers. Curiosity pricked at her, fueled by her earlier thoughts of him and Devlin's mother. Patrick had kept himself away from her over the past week, only making her more eager to know about him. Although that was probably the opposite of his intentions.

"Devlin looks just like him," she offered.

Seamus nodded with a smile. "That he does." He reached across the table to grab on to her hand. "I pray you can help him, lass."

For the flash of a moment she knew he didn't speak of Devlin. But why on earth would Patrick need her help? "Y-yes," she stammered. "So do I."

Seamus didn't say anything more, not about Patrick or Devlin. The sun beckoned through the wide windows, and she chose to turn her mind to other thoughts. One glance at Devlin showed her he, too, felt the pull of the beautifully-landscaped backyard. His eyes were opened wide as he stared toward the springtime colors visible beyond the window.

"I believe we'll head outside now," she said brightly. Devlin didn't respond, but his shoulders tightened. "Come, Devlin."

At Seamus's nod she helped Devlin down from his chair and gently pulled him by the hand through the French doors that opened into the backyard. He followed on stiff legs.

But he followed.

***

Patrick made his way back home, eager to see Devlin. And, he could admit to himself, eager to see Tara. Over the past week, since that awkward moment at breakfast when

he'd felt the pull of her, he'd kept his distance. He could hear
her, moving around in her room, washing in the water closet. He
could smell her in his room, her sweet scent lingering after she'd
seen to Devlin. She filled his senses, and he had no right to feel
anything for her except gratitude.

But he'd watched her working with his son, without her
knowledge. Sadly, he'd seen little progress. It was clear she
cared for the boy. And Devlin was growing attached to her, as
attached as the troubled boy could be. He guessed Tara saw
Devlin's tiny reactions to her presence. The boy was as attracted
to Tara as the father was. Little wonder, that. She was as bright
as sunshine through the thick trees bordering the dell.

What would happen when he took Tara home, when her
treatment with Devlin was finished? He shook his head. He
wouldn't think about that. He would continue to pray that she
brought the little boy back and whole. She was as dedicated to
Devlin as he had seen her with that little girl at the hospital. And
if her success meant her leaving the dell, so be it. For once in his
young life, Devlin would have to come first.

Steeling himself against his attraction to Tara, he stepped up
onto the stoop and entered the house.

"Oh, we weren't expectin' ya, Master Patrick," Mrs.

O'Grady called through the archway to the dining room. She straightened and walked into the parlor. "Miss Tara and the lad already had luncheon."

Disappointment flicked at him, but he pushed it aside. "Ah."

"They're outside in the gardens," she offered.

He didn't miss the anticipation on the old woman's face.

Seeking to hide his own, he nodded. "Thank you, Mrs. O'Grady."

Patrick walked through the house to the find Tara and Devlin in the gardens, playing catch with a ball on the flagstone walk. Well, she was playing and he was watching. Closely. Devlin kept his head down, apparently studying the veining and colors set in the stones beneath him. But Patrick didn't miss his eager gaze each time the ball rolled close to him. Devlin's body tensed, almost invisibly.

Tara laughed and talked to the child, keeping up both sides of their conversation. As when he'd seen her before in the behavior lab, Patrick marveled that anyone could ignore her. And now, to hear her lilting eager voice, he was amazed his son didn't burst through his walls and throw himself into her arms. The good Lord knew Patrick yearned to do just that. Instead Patrick held himself as still as Devlin, forcing himself to be content to watch for the moment.

Tara was so graceful as she moved in the garden. With the sun glinting off her hair and a bright smile on her face, she was achingly lovely. The pretty day dress she wore caught the gentle breeze, now and then outlining her fetching curves. Again, he stiffened and fought her lure.

She laughed out loud again, the sound throaty and free. A sensation struck him straight in the belly and he sucked in a breath. He recognized it for what it was. Lust.

"Nay," he rasped, stepping back.

Tara didn't deserve his attentions. She was pure and good and he wouldn't let his sin touch her. Devlin stood there, still immobile and off-kilter in the dappled shade of one large tree. Patrick's shoulders slumped as his ardor cooled. His sin had done this to Devlin. He'd be damned if his passions ruined Tara as well.

Without a word to either Tara or the boy, he went back into the house to gather his things. He had to get out of there and fast. He would move into the workshop. Keep himself from his home and family. Devlin was in Tara's capable hands. The boy would

get well without his interference. And Tara would be safe
without his attentions.

He began to pull some clothes out of the wardrobe, his
body's yearnings still driving him.

"It's for the best," he muttered, grabbing up an extra
pair of boots. "It's not as if it'll be forever." He stuffed his
belongings into a satchel. "They'll have to understand."

"Are you daft, lad?"

Patrick stopped, his brush and comb in hand, and
glanced over his shoulder. His uncle stood in the doorway,
his bushy brows low over his eyes.

Patrick shook his head and continued to pack his
satchel. "I'll stay at the workshop for the time-being, Uncle.
It's best."

Seamus snorted and stepped into the room. "And
what'll the little laddie think?"

Patrick froze. Devlin was more aware of Patrick since
first coming to the dell. And now and again he faced Patrick
with a clarity in his gaze that struck him straight through to
his heart. No matter. Tara and Devlin didn't need him there.

"He'll have Tara, Uncle," he said. "She's the one to
help him."

"So you keep sayin'," Seamus answered. "Since you snatched her and brought her here."

Patrick ignored the guilt niggling at the back of his mind and turned his back on his uncle. "Aye."

"But what about when she leaves?" Seamus asked. "Where will the boy be then?"

"Tara's not leaving," Patrick said.

Damn. He knew the moment the words left his mouth his uncle wouldn't hesitate to leap on them.

Confirming Patrick's thoughts, Seamus grunted. "That's the way of it, then," the old man said in a low voice. "I knew it."

Patrick closed his satchel and finally turned to face Seamus.

"What?" he growled. "What, pray, do you think you know?"

Seamus glanced toward the open bedroom door before leaning closer to Patrick. Patrick braced himself.

"You favor the lass," Seamus said.

"Nay, Uncle."

"'Tis no shame to admit it."

Shame? Ah, there was that. Patrick raked his fingers through his hair, his anger fleeing. "She deserves better than a sinner like myself."

"But she can help you, lad. Don't you see what's right

before you?"

Aye. He could see Tara clearly in his mind's eye. A sweet lass with a strong spirit. Suddenly, the marks on his shoulder began to throb, a stark reminder of all that came before. Of what would stay with him forever.

"It's not meant to be," he said. "Pray, don't speak of it again."

Seamus's mouth turned down slightly and his green eyes were dark. "As you wish, lad. I only want what's best for Devlin. And for you."

"Tara's best for Devlin." Patrick picked up his bag and walked toward the doorway. "And neither of them need me here."

His uncle said nothing more.

Patrick gave a nod. "I'll be back to get some of my things now and again."

"Aye," Seamus sighed. "And I'm sure Mrs. O'Grady won't let ya' go hungry when you drop by."

Patrick offered a small smile at that. He left the house, bound for the workshop.

And his solitary penance.

Chapter 10

"Oh, Devlin!" Tara cried. "You almost caught the ball. I'm so proud of you!"

The child faced her, a tiny spark of interest in his big blue eyes. He sat on the low stone wall across from her and, though her back ached from keeping the position, she still bent over and rolled the ball toward him. She felt like she'd been at this for hours. A glance at her watch told her that wasn't quite true, but she stood and stretched anyway.

"What do you say to having some of Mrs. O'Grady's biscuits, Devlin?"

The boy scrambled to his feet. Tara's heart leaped but she refrained from grabbing him to her and smothering him with kisses.

She simply nodded and held out her hand. "Come, sweetheart. I can almost taste those biscuits now."

Devlin took her hand, his fingers slack but warm in her hand nonetheless. Her fatigue and aching back forgotten, Tara beamed a smile at the boy and led him back into the house. His uneven gait didn't match hers, but he followed.

Mrs. O'Grady was in the kitchen, humming and fussing about. Tara called a greeting to her and sat Devlin down at the table.

Mrs. O'Grady peeped out of the kitchen. "Oh, the little mite be hungry then?"

"Yes, Mrs. O'Grady," Tara answered.

She watched as Devlin held himself straight on his pile of books on the chair. She knew he recognized the way they comported themselves at the table and mimicked the motion. Pride swelled within her, pride for all he'd accustomed himself to since she'd arrived.

"Devlin would like a few of your fine biscuits." Tara mimicked the boy's posture. "Wouldn't you, Devlin?"

Tara saw it then, a tiny nod of the boy's head. She nearly shouted with the joy of it. He just communicated!

Mrs. O'Grady didn't see the small miracle as she left the dining room, but Tara took it for what it was. Real progress. Tears pricked her eyes but she blinked them away before the child could see them. She couldn't wait to tell Patrick.

"Isn't Master Patrick comin' in, Miss Tara?" the housekeeper asked.

Tara started, and wondered if Mrs. O'Grady was blessed with second sight to read Tara's thoughts. "From where?" she asked.

The woman peered behind her toward the backyard. She clicked her tongue and turned toward the kitchen. "Guess he took himself back to the workshop, then."

With that, she left Devlin and Tara in the dining room. Why did Mrs. O'Grady think Patrick would join them for a snack? She looked out the French doors and saw no one in the yard. Certainly no Patrick, standing in the dappled sunshine eager to share their work.

She smiled at Devlin and set his father from her mind. She and Devlin shared a few cookies that were fragrant with cinnamon as she mentally composed her notes. After their snack, the child went down for a nap in his little bed. Though he stirred quite a bit, he fell asleep after about five minutes. Tara went to her room to update her notes. And to anticipate the moment she would tell Patrick that his son was coming back to his family. To his father.

That evening, Tara fixed her hair to better suit the pretty yellow dress she'd changed into. Mrs. O'Grady took good care of Brianna's dresses, but if Tara hadn't creased and rumpled today's blue dress she wouldn't have bothered changing for dinner. She had no clue how to use hairpins, but thankfully

Brianna had sent over some clips. Plastic, she saw without surprise. Brianna was amazing.

She swept her hair off her neck and fastened the clip at her crown. "Not bad," she said to her reflection.

She couldn't deny it. She was eager to see Patrick. He was so worried about his son, and if she could give him a bit of hope she wouldn't hesitate. That she found him the most attractive man she'd ever seen didn't matter. She smirked at herself and left her room. *Yeah, right.*

When she arrived in the dining room Sean was already standing there, a charming MacDonald grin on his face. He was as broad as Patrick, and very handsome. But he wasn't Patrick.

"Good evenin', Miss Tara," he said with a bow.

"Good evening, Sean," she said.

Tara inclined her head and looked for Patrick.

"'Tis just me this evenin'," Sean offered. "And my uncle and nephew, of course."

Tara turned to find Seamus leading Devlin into the room. The boy stared up at his great-uncle, though little else showed his awareness. His features were blank, his mouth set. But she glimpsed a similarity between the two of them, one she hadn't noticed before.

Seamus had a sparkle of something, an air of crackling energy around him. But Devlin... Again, she saw a touch of something uncanny about the boy.

"Patrick's stayin' at the workshop," Sean said, interrupting her strange thoughts.

She saw Devlin look toward the door and felt his disappointment herself. Had she imagined the longing on his little face?

"Oh?" she asked, keeping her voice even for the child's sake.

Sean opened his mouth to say more, but a quelling look from his uncle stilled him. He stood there, his hands held stiffly at his side.

"'Tis kind of you to set aside your questions, lass," Seamus said. "But my daft nephew... Ah, let's not speak of it now."

He perched Devlin on his chair beside her and they began their meal. Sean settled his big frame across from Tara after she took her seat.

Sean was a lively dinner partner. Charming, and very attentive and bright.

"You looked lovely tonight, Miss Tara," Sean said.

Seamus cleared his throat and again Sean grew quiet. But a smile teased Sean's generous mouth, and Tara smiled in return.

"Thank you, Sean," she said. "Brianna's dresses are just so pretty, I'm sure they take the credit."

There was a spark of something in Sean's green eyes, a masculine appreciation she hadn't seen in years. Even Mark had never looked at her like that, like she was the only person in the room. But she missed Patrick, both his speaking to his son and sharing warm glances with her. Sean's bright green eyes were nothing compared to the memory of Patrick's brooding blue-gray ones.

"Devlin almost caught the ball today," she announced.

"Did ya' now?" Seamus asked the boy with a grin. "Soon you'll be playin' with your uncles, I wager. And your cousin Bryce."

Devlin eyed the man and Tara believed he longed to speak to him. His mouth quivered but still he said nothing.

"And tomorrow we're going for a walk," she said.

"A walk?" Sean asked. "Where, pray?"

She shrugged. "Around the village. It looks utterly charming."

Sean shook his head, his black brows drawn together. "Nay, Tara. 'Tis unwise to go about the dell."

Tara began to voice her objections when she caught Seamus's gaze.

The old man gave a slow nod. "The people in the dell, lass," he began. "They... Devlin's new here, is all."

Sean lowered his voice as he leaned closer to Tara. "Aye, when we went to church last Sunday more than one person said to make sure the little devil stays away."

Tara felt anger simmer in her belly. The ignorant residents of the dell still believed the boy a devil? Patrick had told her that much, but still?

"Of all the narrow-minded..." She couldn't finish her thought, her throat tight with the unfairness of it all. Devlin was watching her so closely, she didn't dare voice her anger at the petty villagers.

"You speak the truth of it, aye," Patrick's uncle said. "But there it be."

She nodded, turning a bright smile on Devlin. "Why, we'll just have to content ourselves in the backyard, Devlin. It's a lovely yard, isn't it? The pretty green trees and the lovely flowers growing along the walk."

The boy said nothing, just chewed mechanically on a piece of Mrs. O'Grady's fresh bread. She was relieved to see he didn't recognize the prejudice. No child should have to feel like an outsider. The sting of that rejection still struck her now and then.

More than ever she wanted to bring him out of himself, to show the outsiders that he was worthy and good. Tears choked her throat.

"I'll come and play with you, Devlin," Sean said. "That is, if Miss Tara doesn't mind."

Tara started. The interest on Sean's face wasn't threatening, but she was still uncomfortable with the man's attentions. This was amazing, since whenever Patrick looked at her so intently she only felt pleasantly warm.

"That would be nice," she said at last.

Her gaze fell on Patrick's empty chair. Why did he stay away? Was he angry with her? Did he distrust her therapy?

She followed Devlin's lead and ate her food in silence, her mind working.

***

Patrick set aside his plate, empty now of its bread and cheese and cold meat. He could well guess the meal served

148

in their house right now. Some of Mrs. O'Grady's fine fare would serve him quite nicely. But Tara would be there as well, more tempting than anything set before him on the table. Again, lust licked along his nerves. He would keep to the workshop. He would keep to himself. 'Twas best for everyone.

The place had been busy this afternoon, which was a blessing in itself. Time and again he had seen Tara in his mind, so lovely and sweet there in the sunlight. And Devlin, so still in spite of her encouragement, standing in the shadows. Would the girl reach through to him? He prayed so. For not only would Devlin have a chance at a real life, but Tara would go back to Indianapolis and live her own life. She would be safe then, without the danger Patrick would cause no matter how hard he tried to separate from her.

He ran his fingers over his scarred shoulder, and felt the skin pucker and burn. Aye, her leaving would be for the best. He dropped his hand and fisted it. Then why, pray, did his heart feel like it was ripping in two?

***

Tara walked through the dell, stopping at the pretty little shops and nodding greetings to the people who watched her so closely. She'd been here for nearly three weeks now, and her borrowed dresses and shoes seemed as comfortable as her abandoned jeans and sneakers. As nice as Seamus's house was, it was good to get out on her own.

These walks had become a routine for her over the past few days, giving her the opportunity to be alone with her thoughts. She longed to bring Devlin on her walks, but she agreed with Seamus that doing so would expose him to the irrational fears of the people here. The folks here were narrow-minded people, unable to see the scared little boy hidden deep inside Devlin.

The butcher peered at her out the wide window at the front of his store, his mouth set in a grim line. She stared openly at him, daring him to step out of his shop and give voice to the venom she could read in his eyes. As she passed the blacksmith's she heard the pounding hammer still and felt the man's eyes on her back. Another dose of negativity sent her way. Did they watch her because she was helping Devlin? Or was it because she dared to walk through the village without escort?

"Too stinkin' bad," she muttered to herself.

She had no clue about the social rules of this time, this place. And what was more, she didn't care.

She never hesitated to walk around Indianapolis by herself. She wasn't going to let these old-fashioned people dictate her actions. Smiling at her choice of words, she shook her head. She was a woman of the future. A woman of her own mind. The people here in the dell were at home as she never would be. As incongruous it should seem, the thought filled her with a pang of longing.

The dress shop was ahead, the one place she felt comfortable in the dell other than Seamus's house and gardens. The woman who owned the store was pleasant, and reminded Tara of Mrs. O'Grady. She was very matter-of-fact but friendly, and had only nice things to say. Tara pushed open the door and stepped into the cool interior, the crisp scent of clean linens and lemon oil reaching her.

"Good afternoon, Miss Tara!" the dressmaker called.

Tara smiled at the little brown-haired lady, her expression the first she'd dared to show on her face since leaving the house to walk through the dell.

"Hello, Mrs. McKay," she answered.

Two women who looked younger than Tara stood in the store, running their fingers over the ribbons draped along one wall. She'd seen them in the dell before, though they kept to the other side of the street whenever she passed. They were pretty girls, with blond hair and fair skin, and looked enough alike to be sisters. They ran their pale blue eyes over Tara and she felt a chill dance over his skin.

They both clicked their tongues and faced each other. "There be the MacDonalds's guest," one of them said, her voice sneering on the last word.

Her meaning wasn't lost on Tara, though as a modern woman she shouldn't care about her supposedly-tainted reputation.

"Yes," she answered, stepping closer to the pair. "I'm staying with the MacDonalds."

The girls continued as if Tara hadn't spoken, merely flicking their eyes at her for a second.

"She's pretty enough, I wager," the second girl put in. "Surely Patrick MacDonald brought her here for his own dark reasons."

Tara began to turn away, knowing she could say nothing to halt their gossip. People here were no different than in the future, eager for gossip and ignorant of the pain they could cause. She half expected to see a hateful post on Facebook, if it existed in this time and place.

"Aye," the first said with a smirk. "'Tis a pity she spends her days with that horrid little—"

"Shut your mouth!" Tara said through clenched teeth. She whirled on them, her hands in fists. "Say what you will about me, I don't care. But Devlin is an innocent child. What is wrong with you people?"

Both girls faced her, their lovely faces wearing ugly scowls that struck Tara with their true poison.

"The changeling be Patrick MacDonald's punishment," the first girl said with a nod.

"'Tis true," the other added. "Ask anyone in the dell."

Tara took in a deep breath and let it out, silently praying for control in the face of such prejudice.

"I know Devlin," she began. "He's sweet and smart and worthy of love."

The first girl laughed, a sickening sound filled with no humor. "How can you say such silliness?" she asked. "Why, the boy's mother was a—"

"That's enough," Mrs. McKay said.

The three young women all turned to face the storekeeper. Mrs. McKay met Tara's startled gaze with one of understanding and Tara felt the fight leave her. The MacDonalds had one ally here, but she was a formidable one.

"Humph," the second girl began. "Let's go home, Mary. There is nothing here I'd want to purchase."

"Aye," her sister smirked. "The wares have dimmed in quality, I daresay."

With that parting shot, the two girls swept out of the store. Tara let out a breath to ease her anger, closing her eyes for a long moment. At last she felt herself cool and turned to the shopkeeper.

"I'm so sorry, Mrs. McKay," Tara began.

"Don't be worryin' about those two witches, Miss Tara," Mrs. McKay said with a wink. "I have the only dress shop in the dell. They'll be back."

"But when they spoke of Devlin that way." She couldn't put her thoughts into words at the moment.

"Aye. Dorothy O'Grady told me of yer work with the boy." The woman stepped closer to place a caring hand on Tara's arm. "And of yer affection."

Tara nodded, grateful once more for Mrs. O'Grady's support. "He's not a devil."

"How could he be?" Mrs. McKay smiled. "He's a MacDonald."

"But what they said." Tara blew a tendril of hair off her face with a puff of air. "Why do they think he's evil?"

Mrs. McKay shook her head. "Don't you be listenin' to their tales, Miss Tara. You have the right of it."

Tara knew the lady was right, and couldn't be more relieved to have a vocalization of her own feelings. Devlin was good, and both her mind and her heart recognized it. There was the mystery of the boy's mother, but surely if those girls really knew her identity they wouldn't hesitate to blurt it out to Tara.

"What have you got to show me today, Mrs. McKay?" Tara asked, eager to abandon the subject at hand.

The lady beamed and withdrew a large book of patterns and Tara indulged her newfound hobby of studying Regency fashions.

***

"I need a new pair of dance slippers," a girl's voice said.

Patrick looked up from his workbench to see the two yellow-haired chits from the dell. They stood in the front of the shop, their faces wearing identical pouts. What the devil? The silly girls never came to the shop, preferring to send their lady's maid to buy a few pairs that may or may not catch their fancy.

On his guard, he wiped his hands on a rag and listened

closely as Sean spoke to them.

"Aye," his brother said. "We have some of the softest slippers, miss."

They giggled, the sound grating on Patrick's ears.

"Soft slippers made by such manly hands?" one of them cooed.

"Such big hands," the other girl put in.

Patrick stepped toward to the front, his eyes narrowed. What was their game now? He looked at Sean to see his brother basking in the feminine attention, his grin wide.

"MacDonalds make the best shoes, miss," Sean beamed. "'Tis our pride in our work."

"Hmm," one of the blond girls said. "Such dedication. Do you think we should purchase something, Carrie?"

"Oh, I don't know Mary," the other blond said. "What do you think?"

The other clicked her tongue. "MacDonald shoes are the best, Carrie. That's what Mama says."

Sean laughed and gave a nod, his chest puffed out.

"Aye," he said again. "And nothin' but the best for your delicate feet, I wager."

That was enough. Patrick walked into the room and

held himself still. "I haven't seen you two ladies in the shop before."

They both ran their gazes over him, their pale eyes cold. Together they lifted their chins.

"Sean MacDonald," the first one began, her back to Patrick. "My sister and I saw that guest of yours at Mrs. McKay's dress shop."

"Tara?" Sean asked.

Patrick winced. *Shut up, Sean.* The fool was playing right into their hands.

"Is that her name?" the second girl asked, her eyes wide. "Pretty girl. But not terribly pleasant."

"Aye, sister. Quite rude, she was. Why, all we did was ask after that little boy of Patrick MacDonald's, and—"

"I'll wager you did!" Patrick growled. "What did you say to Tara, you witch?"

"Witch?" The girl laughed. "Fancy you callin' me a witch when you laid down with a Banshee!"

Patrick took a step toward them, but Sean put a hand on his arm.

"Easy, brother." He turned to the girls, his teasing grin gone now. "My nephew is a MacDonald. 'Twould serve you well to

157

remember that."

They both blinked at Sean's rebuff. The older of the
two girls bristled.

"Well! I see there's a streak of rudeness in the
MacDonald house."

"Get out," Patrick said. "And don't let me hear you
spreadin' any of your lies about my son. Or about Tara."

The two girls left the shop, their heads together as they
giggled and snickered.

"Bloody harridans," Patrick muttered.

"'Tis only gossip, Patrick."

Patrick shook his head. "They could do a fair amount of
damage with their sharp tongues, Sean. To us, aye. But to
Tara and Devlin most of all."

Sean smiled once more, his easy nature clearly restored.
"Devlin has Tara to protect him, Patrick. Surely she's
stronger than anythin' those witches could say."

Patrick knew Sean was right, at least where Tara was
concerned. And from what little those girls said, he knew
Tara had defended the boy as if he were her own.

It wouldn't raise her in Patrick's eyes, though. He knew
what she was made of already. He'd suspected her strong

spirit and loyal heart back in Indianapolis. She was good for Devlin. Good for all of them, he'd wager. He stilled once more.

"Aye," Patrick conceded. Sean opened his mouth, no doubt to say more about Tara, but he held up one hand. "I best be getting' back to work."

He walked back to his workbench, swallowing the bitterness the two girls had spread. They were indeed witches, and as vile as any Banshee.

"Your work," he heard Sean mutter. "Your escape, more like."

Patrick said nothing to that.

Chapter 11

Tara sat in Brianna's kitchen, watching Bryce scribble in a suspiciously-modern coloring book as his mother prepared some tea. And though he only had a handful of crayons, countless colors appeared on the page.

"That's very good, Bryce," she said, peering at the picture. "Those are some very unusual colors."

Bryce nodded, a wide smile on his face as he shot her a glance out of the corner of his eye. "I make them up!"

To show her what he meant, he blinked his eyes and the crayon in his hand changed color. Tara stared as the child went back to his work. Surely she was seeing things. The boy didn't just turn that crayon from yellow to a delicate shade of blue the color of a robin's egg!

Brianna set a tea cup before Tara and looked over Bryce's shoulder. "Oh, love! That's quite—"

Her eyes went round and she shot a look at Tara. Pink colored her cheeks as she spread her hands.

"I suppose you have some questions for me?" Brianna asked.

Tara gulped. "I don't quite know."

"I should've told you." Brianna smiled, settling into a

chair beside her son. "We're magic," she said simply.

Tara gaped at her and Bryce. They looked so normal. Well, it was true the woman traveled to the future and back. Tara had managed somehow to wrap her head about that bit of truth. But, magic?

"H-how?"

Brianna looked at her. an indulgent expression softening her pretty face. "We're Cornish Pixies, Tara."

She held her hand over her mouth. *Whoa.*

Brianna nodded. "It's true."

Tara saw that quality about Bryce then, that otherworldliness she had glimpsed in Devlin. Did that mean Devlin was magic, too?

"And Devlin?" she had to know. "Is Patrick's son also magic?"

"Not how you're supposing," Brianna said quickly. "The MacDonalds aren't from Cornwall."

Tara clicked her tongue. "That's not what I meant, Brianna. Is Devlin also magic?"

The worry creasing Brianna's brow caused a flutter in Tara's belly.

"Look, Tara," Brianna said. "It's not my place to speak of

the MacDonalds to you. Patrick should be the one to tell you."

"But they're magic, too?"

Brianna laughed, a shot of warmth in their odd conversation. "Oh, not like you're thinking. But they *are* blessed with a heavy dose of charm."

Bryce looked up as if on cue and Tara could swear she saw a sparkle in his eyes. She pulled back, blinking rapidly. She suddenly remembered that long-ago talk with Patrick in the Children's Hospital, recalling the warmth that had filled her then. Her mind had been confused and her tongue loose. And hadn't he found her apartment with no trouble? The realization struck her hard.

"Then Patrick…" She put her head in her hands. "He charmed me?"

Brianna shrugged. "It's their gift, Tara. And if Patrick hadn't been so desperate to bring you here, he never would've used it that way."

"Huh!"

But Tara couldn't summon any real anger at the man, not knowing now what she did about Devlin.

Brianna touched her hand. "Your work with Devlin,

Tara," she began. "It's a kind of magic too, isn't it?"

Now it was Tara's turn to shrug. There was something she longed to ask, to find out what was at the center of Devlin's troubles. His progress was indeed accelerated, in her opinion. Like nothing she'd ever encountered. And yet?

She couldn't ask about the boy's mother, not with Bryce sitting there. The image of the smirking girls from the dress shop was still fresh in her mind. She drained her tea cup and stood.

"Thank you for the tea, Brianna. I should go." She ruffled Bryce's auburn curls. "See you later, Bryce."

The little boy grinned, the light reflecting off his perfect white teeth. She blinked again. How could she have missed it? MacDonald charm.

Luke MacDonald came in then, a smile on his handsome face for his wife and son. He stopped when he saw Tara, and nodded his head in greeting.

"Hello, Tara."

"Hello, Luke," she returned.

He turned to kiss Brianna and then tickled Bryce beneath his chin.

Feeling out of place, and a little envious of the family's obvious affection, Tara began to turn from the scene. "Well, I'd better get back to Devlin."

"I hear you're workin' a miracle with the boy, Tara," Luke said. He grinned as brightly as his son. "Uncle Seamus says you're more valuable than all the Macdonald gold."

Gold? What the heck? Tara's head began to spin.

"Luke," she heard Brianna say. "Tara doesn't know."

Luke's green eyes widened. "Ah, lass. I'm sorry."

Tara slumped back down in her chair. It all made sense now. Seamus's burly stature and shock of bright red hair, his fondness for green clothing, the charm all the MacDonalds had in such abundance. And now gold?

"The MacDonalds," she began. "You're all Leprechauns?"

"Braunachs," Brianna corrected.

Tara let the information settled. "Braunachs? What's a Braunach?"

Brianna nodded. "Their akin to Leprechauns, but bear very little physical resemblances."

Tara through for a second. Yeah, she couldn't see any of the tall and strong MacDonalds on a box of Lucky Charms. "But, how can Braunachs be so…?"

"Handsome," Luke teased.

She laughed and shook her head, coming to her feet again. "No. I mean, they are. You are." She waved one hand through the air, giving up the battle. "I must get back to Devlin. A Braunach?" The three of them nodded. "Braunachs."

"Do call again, Tara," Brianna said, walking her to the front door. "I enjoy the company."

Tara absently smiled and nodded her agreement. She walked out onto the wide street bisecting the dell, ignoring the stares and slights she received from the people there. Her mind worked around the puzzle of Devlin's trouble.

The whole Braunach thing made no real difference. So none of them were quite human, then? Maybe that helped to explain why Devlin was progressing so quickly in some areas but not so in others. Why the heck not? She'd given up any hope of rational thought when she'd accepted that she was now in the year 1814. To let this knowledge color her perceptions of Devlin and his family would make her no better than the narrow-minded shrews in the village. Devlin needed her, and it didn't matter if he was different. Or "normal" for here and now.

She turned down the lane toward Seamus's house and thought about Devlin. When she caught the child's gaze now and then, clear and bright, it was as if there was something else inside of him. Something that held on to his soul with an iron grip. He was a Braunach. A small Braunach, but Tara knew little of the legend. Apparently they were tall and strong, but akin to Leprechauns. Were they mischievous? Not as much as she'd seen. They did all appear to be charming to a fault, though. She thought about Patrick again. Charming to a definite fault.

She was pleased with Devlin's progress so far, as it exceeded anything in her experience before Patrick brought her here. But that was strange in itself. She needed to speak to Patrick. But that man had kept himself from her and his family for nearly a month now. Why?

Devlin looked for his father every night when Sean came back from the workshop alone. And though the little boy paid close attention to everything said at the table now, Tara didn't miss that his keen gaze repeatedly settled on Patrick's empty chair. As her own often did. Well, in her defense he was a big man to miss. He left a large space in his absence.

Devlin was troubled, yes. But Patrick had issues as well. His family loved him. That was clear. Seamus was a caring and wonderful patriarch. She didn't know her own father, but she hoped he would've been half as loving as Patrick's uncle was if he'd stuck around. And hadn't she seen the MacDonalds generously shower Devlin with that same affection?

"I don't know." She turned away from the lane and gazed at the woods. Sun dappled and inviting, the needle-strewn path drew her. "I can't go home right now."

She flinched at the easy way she used the word "home" to describe Seamus's cottage. She didn't have a home. Not really. Not here in the dell. And certainly not back in Indianapolis. A chill tickled her belly even as a prick of heat stung her eyes. She sniffed, forcing her mind from thoughts of home. Any home.

The weather was warm and the day was bright. She'd walk into the lovely woods set not far from the edge of the dell and focus on nothing more than the clean scent of the trees and flowers.

***

Patrick stood at his workbench, staring out the window and seeing nothing but Tara before him. He'd heard from his uncle of her progress with Devlin. It amazed him still. The boy didn't speak to anyone yet, true. But he nodded or shook his head in response to questions. Surely that was something! And it was all due to Tara's own particular magic.

Both his uncle and his bloody brother spoke glowingly of Tara. Of her grace and spirit and heart. He didn't need their endorsements. He'd known the moment he saw her at the Children's Hospital that she had her own brand of magic. Her work with the children, her compassion, her skill. No, he didn't need Sean's besotted endorsements any more than he needed his uncle's obvious disapproval of Patrick's absence.

Keeping from the house made his days pass easier. His nights were a different matter, however. He couldn't sleep without her crowding his dreams. After seeing her play with Devlin that day in the gardens, he went back to the house again and again to watch them in secret. His son was a miracle to him. How could one poor creature be so cursed by his mother and so loved by Tara?

Patrick hadn't spoken to Devlin since bringing Tara here. Hell, he hadn't really touched the boy except to ruffle his hair a few times since that night when he'd made his promise. But that promise had brought Tara here, someone to give Devlin the attention he wouldn't and the affection he couldn't.

He couldn't help but wonder what it would be like to feel Tara's attention, that warm regard, himself. To see Tara's lovely eyes sparkling with passion, her body pressed tightly against his as they both found fulfillment.

In his dreams he relived that moment he'd held her in his arms. But instead of releasing her in embarrassment he kept her there, learning all the secrets of her eager body.

His skin suddenly felt hot and his clothes were too tight. He sucked in a breath and let it out in a rush. "Bloody fool!"

"What's troublin' you today, Patrick?" Sean looked at him, one brow arched. "As if I couldn't guess."

Patrick raked his fingers through his hair. "Don't start with me, Sean."

"You're the one livin' here by yourself, brother," Sean countered. "Bloody fool, is right."

"What do you know of it, pray?"

Sean threw down his rag and faced him fully. "I know you keep yourself here, like some exile. I know that you want to go to the house. To see your son. To see *her.*"

Patrick's hands clenched into fists, but his anger wasn't toward Sean. Nay, it was directed inward. "I won't talk about this to you," he grumbled.

Sean's mouth thinned to a line, but he said nothing more.

Patrick stalked out the back door and headed for the woods. To the place of his sin. At least he had hope he could escape his wicked thoughts there. He could howl up at the trees. He could pray to God for forgiveness. He had to find relief. Somehow.

***

Tara heard the muttered profanities, the thrashing around in the woods just ahead of her. She trembled, her mouth going dry. There was something familiar about the timbre of that cursing voice. She glanced about the woods, seeing nothing but trees and underbrush and gnarled roots as she had the past half hour. And yet there was something familiar about these particular trees and underbrush and gnarled roots. Then she saw it up ahead. The clearing! She was near the clearing where Patrick first took her after that crazy time jump or whatever it was.

She rested one hand against a tree's rough bark and held herself still, waiting to hear that grumbling voice again. Her heart raced as she held her breath.

"Bloody stupid bastard!"

Her heart slowed its rapid beat as she recognized the man's voice. Patrick.

She pushed away from the tree, her heart racing for a different reason now. As she stepped into the clearing she saw him, pulling at his hair and hitting himself in the chest.

"Weak-willed, rutting pig!" he cursed.

More profanity, accompanied by odd curses she'd never heard before, spilled from his anger-twisted mouth as he paced. He was like a madman. Or a wounded animal. Fear and longing warred within her. She sensed a sadness clinging to him beneath the anger. Then she glimpsed the track of tears on his cheeks and felt his hopelessness to her soul.

"Lust-driven, son-of-a—"

"Patrick," she called.

He whirled on her, his blue eyes wild, and she stumbled back a step.

Recognition soon settled on his face. He blinked rapidly and took a step toward her. "Tara?" Suddenly he turned away to shake his head. "Get out of here, Tara. Leave me!"

Tara saw it then. That same something she had glimpsed in Devlin's eyes in those brief lucid moments.

She held herself still again, refusing to give in to the urge to run from these woods. To run from him. Using all the skills she'd honed over her years of study, she gathered her knowledge and strength around herself. A gentle yet firm touch. That's what was needed.

"Patrick, please," she said.

He grunted, shaking his head. He raked his fingers through his hair, leaving the red-gold strands standing on end. "It's no place for you, Tara. Not here with me."

He turned from her, leaning one arm against a tree as his breath came fast. She looked at him then, taking in the scuffed boots, the rumpled clothes. He'd been out here for some time, pacing and cursing himself. But, why?

Something pulled her closer to him despite his words to the contrary. He touched her heart as his son did, touched a place that even the children in Indianapolis never had.

Tara stepped closer and gently touched his left shoulder.

Patrick let out a howl and twisted away from her.

"Leave me, Tara!" he shouted again. "You don't know what you're playin' at here."

She licked her lips and shook her head. She couldn't leave if she wanted to. Not now.

172

"Let me help you."

His face showed his anguish, and his hope, that she could somehow help him. But still he shook his head. "Nay."

"Tell me what's wrong, Patrick. Please."

He pulled back and froze. She thought he would leave her but in the next moment he reached for her, grabbed her tightly to him. He moved his mouth close to hers. Her pulse raced at the close contact, with fear or passion she couldn't guess. She could smell him, could almost taste him, and her body flushed with wanting.

"Tara, lass…"

He brushed his lips against hers, sucking in a breath as if he couldn't live without her kiss. Her heart began to pound again, desire filling every inch of her. She returned his kiss, welcoming his tongue when it begged entry.

She'd never been kissed like this, like her soul had been starving for something that only now was given to her. His hands moved over her back, her bottom, and she leaned closer to him.

The next moment he shoved her away, leaving her gasping for air.

"What's wrong?" she asked on a breath.

"You want to know what's wrong?" He faced her, his lips

curled. "I'll show you what's wrong!" He pulled at his shirt, tugging it out of his waistband. "I'll show you, damn it."

He tore off his shirt and for a moment she could only stare at his magnificent upper body, his broad shoulders. Curls of golden hair swirled lightly over his chest, his flat belly, and her fingers itched to touch him.

She fisted her hands. "I don't—"

"Look!"

He turned from her and she saw it. Five scars high on his left shoulder blade. Red and angry, and raised to almost look like fingers.

His shoulders slumped. "I'm marked, Tara." The anger was gone from his voice as it broke. "I'm marked as much as Devlin."

She unclenched her hands and reached toward him. She touched the scars and her fingers began to tingle. He sucked in a breath, his big body tensing. With a growl he turned and pulled her to him.

"Tara…"

Chapter 12

Patrick crushed his mouth to Tara's once more, tasting sunlight and purity and passion. Again he parted her lips with his tongue, catching her little moan of pleasure as she gave herself as she had moments earlier. His body hardened and he pressed closer still. Her arms circled his neck and he could feel every curve of her through the thin dress she wore. He cupped her round bottom and pulled her up, cradling his sex against her belly.

"Tara, lass," he moaned.

She answered him with her body, leaning her head back to give him access to her throat. He kissed her there, feeling her racing pulse beneath his tongue.

"Patrick..."

Desire pounded through him, unlike anything he'd experienced before. His body burned, his soul ached. Not even all those times with the Banshee, had passion burned so hot in him.

Guilt slashed through his body and he shoved Tara from him, taking a long gulp of air as his body twitched with unfulfilled cravings. He glanced at Tara, and saw the soft look in her eyes, her kiss-swollen lips.

She held one hand toward him, beckoning. "Patrick?"

"Leave me, Tara," he rasped. She hesitated, her brow creased in obvious confusion. She stepped close to him and he held up one hand. "Leave me. I'm no good for you. No good for anyone."

She shook her head, her sable curls tumbling loose now over her creamy shoulders. Again his body screamed for release. It had been so long.

"Nay!" he cried.

She backed away, her eyes round as she held a hand over her mouth. The next instant she turned and ran, stumbling over tree roots and brush as she took herself from him. From the danger of his passion.

Patrick watched her go, his stomach clenching. He reached up with his right hand, feeling the familiar ridges on his left shoulder. They still burned, and yet they seemed... changed. Thinner. He was going daft! 'Twas a good thing he was living at the workshop. He didn't know what he would do if he caught a glimpse Tara again after holding her so close.

Aye, but she was sweet in her passion. He'd tasted it on her, had felt it in her every motion. His body ached for release, pounding in rhythm with his heartbeat. He prayed Tara made Devlin well and soon. Then he could get her back to Indianapolis.

And away from him.

***

Tara reached the house almost before she knew it. She didn't know if anyone saw her in her mad dash from the woods, and she cared even less.

She took a moment to collect herself on the porch. One hand to her hair told her Patrick had disturbed more than her senses. Her hair was a mess, and she had no clue how to fix it without a mirror. Instead she simply took out the few hairpins left and ran her fingers through the curls.

"Whatever." She glanced down at herself. At least her dress was still relatively straight.

She opened the door and breathed a sigh to find the living room empty.

"Devlin, nay!" she heard Mrs. O'Grady cry.

She ran to the child's room, finding Devlin acting like a wild thing. His grunts and cries filled the room. Mrs. O'Grady stood in the doorway, her wide eyes showing relief as she saw Tara.

"Oh, Miss Tara. Thank God yer here!"

Tara went to Devlin, finding him twitching and pacing as his father had been. No curses came from him, but the anger and self-loathing was evident on his little face and nearly broke her heart.

"Devlin," she said in the same firm, gentle tone she'd use with his father.

The child turned, his eyes focused squarely on her face. Tara felt his gaze as if he touched her, both wild and beseeching. He threw himself at her as she crouched down, his arms wrapped tightly around her neck. He shook with silent sobs, but no real tears wet her skin.

"Easy, sweetheart," she cooed, sinking down to the floor as she cradled him tight. "Easy, Devlin."

The child continued to cry, burrowing against her for comfort her heart was all too happy to give. In all her weeks of working with the child, she had suspected he'd worked his way into her heart. Now she knew she loved him. And this was the first time he'd initiated any physical contact. The first time he'd longed for such a strong connection to another person.

"Easy, sweetheart," she said again, her own tears

adding to his.

"T-ta…"

She stilled. Did he try to say her name? "Yes, Devlin." She held her breath for a moment. "Tara."

"Ta…raaah."

No more words came from him, but she knew she would hold that softly-spoken word in her heart forever.

"I know, love," she said, easily using the common endearment. "I'm here with you and you're okay."

Devlin took in a shuddering breath and nodded his head, his silky curls tickling her cheek.

"Patrick has the right of it, I wager," she heard an awed voice say from the doorway.

She looked up to find Sean standing there, his eyes glistening. Mrs. O'Grady sniffed, a smile on her face. Seamus offered Tara a grin through his own tears.

"Aye, Sean," Seamus added softly, nodding his red head. "Tara's the one."

His words, spoken with such conviction, touched her heart and she tightened her hold on Devlin. The boy sighed, and she felt the tension at last leave his little body. His spirit called to her and she happily surrendered all the tenderness she had within her. She couldn't help but wish she could reach the boy's father as she had the son.

That evening at dinner, Devlin was as silent as always. Yet Tara noticed his eyes continually settled on the people around him. He was coming back to his family. He was making those connections so integral to his recovery. She now believed he wasn't Autistic. No, for no progress she'd ever seen or read about was as startling and sharp as Devlin's.

She took some pride in his progress, because it seemed that all those grants and scholarships hadn't been wasted on her studies. But something inside Devlin, that same something that kept him from his family, was easing its hold on his soul. She just wished she knew why. Then she could make sure it left him forever and he could have the childhood he deserved.

"More bread then, laddie?" Mrs. O'Grady asked the boy.

Devlin didn't nod his head but he looked directly at the woman for a moment. The housekeeper smiled and placed a roll in front of him and stood watching as he began to eat it.

"You like that bread, Devlin," Sean said, taking on

Patrick's Promise ~ JoMarie DeGioia

Tara's mode of addressing the child.

Tara gave him a nod of approval and Sean reddened. But she didn't miss the gaze of affection toward his nephew. Yes. Devlin was coming back to his family. If only his bloody fool of a father could be here to see it.

She started. When had she started to assimilate herself into this place? Into this family? She held her trembling hands flat on the table, her head suddenly light.

"Tara, lass?"

She glanced over to find Patrick's uncle wearing a slight frown.

"Hmm? Yes, Seamus?"

"You be all right, lass? You seem a bit peaked."

She shook her head and offered him a shaky smile. "I'm just tired, I guess."

Devlin stared at her, and she felt his regard to her soul. Before she could stop herself she reached out to tickle him. He froze, but didn't pull away. One corner of his mouth twitched and her heart lifted. She knew the beginnings of a smile if she ever saw one!

"I'm just tired, Seamus," she said again, her eyes still on Devlin. "Gee, I hope I'll be able to tell Devlin some stories

181

tonight."

His little chin bobbed an enthusiastic answer and everyone around the MacDonald table laughed and nodded.

She'd make sure Patrick saw Devlin's improvement firsthand. She was still convinced the man was integral to his son's recovery. How could she ignore the fact that both father and son were wild and sad this afternoon? Braunach were magic, though she knew precious little about them. If she doubted the connection between Patrick and Devlin, there was no denying it now.

Tara finished her meal, telling herself to focus on the child's development instead of his father's apparent deterioration.

***

Patrick sat on the pallet set in one corner of the workshop, his head in his hands. Another sleepless night behind him, he stared at the plank floor and let his mind take the course his dreams had.

Disgust filled him. Why had he touched Tara? She didn't deserve his attentions. She was there for Devlin, and not by her own accord. Nay, he had ripped her from her home and her time to help his son.

But for those brief moments he'd held her? She was good and pure and the promise of redemption was evident in every word. Every movement. Her kisses were sweet and hot and she fit him perfectly. His body reacted as swiftly now as it had in the clearing. Aye, she would be beautiful in her release. Would she cry out his name as she took her pleasure?

He cursed, low and soft. His lust had brought punishment on both him and Devlin. His dark weakness had placed Devlin firmly in the prison of his soul. Nay. Patrick wouldn't let his passions rule him again. He wouldn't take the one pure woman he'd ever met and expose her to that fate.

Luke spoke of Tara often, extolling her virtues by way of his wife's opinions. Patrick knew he shouldn't discount Brianna's views. The Pixie had a way of knowing what was inside people in addition to her own magical talents. And little Bryce had taken to Tara immediately.

He glanced at the clock. At least his work would soon fill his hands if not his head. Sean would add his vocal opinions today, though. But even Sean's baiting wouldn't vex him today. Not if listening to the pup gained him information about Devlin. And Tara.

***

Tara sat in the gardens with Devlin, unable to get the boy's father out of her mind. Another week was behind her and she still made no progress in working through Patrick's problems. Or her feelings for him.

"Ta…ra," Devlin said as he stepped close to her.

She smiled brightly at the boy and wrapped him in her arms. In the past few days he'd called her by her name now and then, earning hugs and kisses and accepting the affection with stoicism. But she was delighted to notice that he didn't pull away from her anymore. She kissed his cheek and quickly released him.

"Go get the ball, Devlin," she instructed.

He stared hard at the ball, intent clear on his face. For a moment she expected the toy to fly into his hands, something his cousin Bryce could probably do without much trouble. But it seemed the only magic Devlin possessed was the ability to wrap her around his finger. She loved the child. And that made Patrick's avoidance all the harder on her.

Devlin picked up the ball and tossed it to her. She had to reach, but she caught it with a whoop of encouragement. The shadow of a smile, though broader than the previous day, she believed, crossed his little face.

He walked to the row of dolls set on the low garden wall and she held her breath. Sean brought them to Tara just yesterday, but she hadn't used them in Devlin's therapy yet. She wanted the child to accustom himself to the representations first.

Sean told her Patrick had made them in the workshop, and the detail on the faces was remarkable. Each soft leather doll represented a member of Devlin's family, down to the little strawberry-blond boy with the solemn features. Devlin picked up the toy child, staring hard at the face.

"That doll looks like you, Devlin," she said, coming to sit beside the dolls on the wall. She picked up the one with brown hair, a young woman she assumed was meant to be her but far prettier than she thought she looked. "And this is me, I think."

Devlin took the doll from her and placed it next to the Devlin doll. "Ta...ra."

"Yes, sweetheart."

He held the two dolls close to his chest with one arm and reached toward the others on the wall. Sean and Patrick were both represented, but he reached toward the stockier image of Seamus. It wore a bright green ribbon, and was the only doll sporting any adornment.

185

"That's Uncle Seamus," she said. "He loves Devlin."

Devlin smiled and gave a slow nod. He touched the Sean doll, running his fingers over the black hair on its head.

"And your Uncle Sean," she said.

He nodded again and held his hand over the Patrick doll. The slight tremble of his hand told her he longed to touch the doll. His little face wore a frown and she felt his reluctance.

"That's your Papa, Devlin," she urged.

He fisted his hand and stepped away from the doll, giving a slight shake of his head. He was angry with Patrick. And visibly hurt. She wouldn't voice those emotions for him today, however. They were too close to her own feelings about the man.

Devlin took the Tara and Devlin dolls and sat on the wall beside her away from the other dolls. He cradled them in his arms as he kept stealing glances at the Patrick doll.

Tara let him have his moment, because they'd been playing outside for nearly an hour. She was relieved to see he still thought of his father, despite the man's long absence. How Patrick could stay away from the child, she couldn't guess. When she went back to Indianapolis, she would miss Devlin terribly. She would have her memories, she supposed. Her mouth quirked. God, would she have her memories.

She knew she'd never forget Patrick's kisses in the clearing. Such passion. Such heat. She fisted her hands in her lap and set it from her mind.

"Come, Devlin," she said, coming to her feet. "It's nearly time for your nap."

Devlin stood and began to gather up his dolls. The Patrick doll still sat on the wall as he turned toward the house. Tara grabbed up the doll and clicked her tongue.

"Patrick MacDonald," she whispered, staring down at the false little face. "Don't you see what you're doing?"

Holding the doll at her side, she followed Devlin into the house.

Chapter 13

Patrick stood in the shadows beyond the garden wall,
his heart pounding. When Tara had spoken his name, so low
and soft, he had nearly run to her. When he saw Devlin
playing with the dolls he'd made, his heart filled with pride.
Sean had asked him on Tara's behalf to make them, for
obviously that lady didn't want anything to do with him
after his behavior in the clearing. But the sight of Devlin's
tiny smile, the halting way he'd said Tara's name, caused
his heart to clench. His son was coming back to them. Well,
to Tara. Not to him. Never to him. Such goodness would
never belong to him.

"I don't deserve the boy," he said to himself.

"Are you daft, lad?"

He whirled to find Seamus perched on the wall behind
him. His uncle wore a frown on his face and Patrick kept his
own features smooth. He gave a cool nod.

"Uncle."

Seamus hopped down and peered up at Patrick. "Did
you see the lass with the boy, Patrick? Did you see the
magic she's makin' right in front of you?"

"He says her name, that's true."

Seamus waved one hand through the air. "That's not all, lad. He's a part of our family now, Patrick. All because of Tara's doin'."

Patrick didn't see any such thing, but he wouldn't argue with his uncle. "If you say so, Uncle."

Seamus grabbed his arm. "Tara is the one, Patrick. She's worth more than all the MacDonald gold!"

Patrick thought of her kisses, of her strong heart and kind soul. "Aye." He shook his head. "But it's not my concern."

Seamus spit out a string of colorful curses. "Damn it, lad! You come here, sneakin' like a thief to see your son. And Tara."

Patrick snorted. "You've been talking to Sean."

Seamus nodded. "Aye. And he's been takin' up your duties where the little lad's concerned. Talkin' to him and playin' with him."

Jealousy pricked at Patrick. He longed to be the one to spend time with Devlin. To teach him things and tell him stories. But it was his own fault, his cowardly defection, and couldn't be helped.

"I'm not needed here."

Seamus rolled his eyes. "Your son needs you, lad. Tara needs you."

"Tara needs nothing from me!"

Seamus blinked in response to his outburst. "What are you sayin', Patrick?"

Patrick raked his fingers through his hair. "Nothing. It's nothing. Tara will help Devlin in her own fashion, Uncle."

He turned and headed back to the workshop.

"Patrick!"

Patrick waved one hand through the air and didn't stop walking.

"You're wrong, lad," he heard Seamus say. "They both need you."

Patrick's heart dared to hope that was true even as his mind told him it couldn't be.

***

Tara ran her fingers over Devlin's hair as the child settled down for sleep. She didn't have to urge him onto the little bed any more, but he still tossed and turned more than she liked.

"Easy, sweetheart," she soothed.

The child let out a breath and rubbed his cheek against his pillow. She let her gaze move over him. He was a Braunach. That explained that odd, charming quality that hung around him. He was a beautiful child, and more like his father than in looks.

The boy held her heart in his little hand. But his father? Patrick reached a part of her she'd never acknowledged before. At the children's home she wasn't exactly showered with affection, though she was treated well enough. Her life in Indianapolis was fulfilling. She shook her head. Her work was really all she had until Patrick brought her here. Now she had connections, brief though they may prove to be. She had a friend in Brianna and enjoyed the company of Mrs. O'Grady and all the MacDonalds. She fit in here far better than she ever had back home. Here with these people, these Braunachs and Pixies, she'd found her place.

Patrick had promised to take her back when Devlin was well. And she cared too much for the little boy to begrudge him his recovery. After those kisses with Patrick in the woods, she knew she'd be better off back in the safety of Indianapolis. Safe. In her little apartment with her fulfilling work at the Children's Hospital.

"Good night, sweetheart," she whispered, dropping a kiss on Devlin's cheek.

She left the child's bedroom and returned to the living room.

Seamus looked up from his book, a pipe held tightly in his teeth. She blinked. A Braunach, to be sure. He smiled at her, his eyes twinkling, and she returned the expression. She picked a book from one of the shelves and settled down on the loveseat.

She wouldn't think about Patrick anymore, she decided as she stared at the words on the page. But she couldn't get the image of him out of her mind, so wild and beautiful there in the woods. And the taste of his fierce kisses.

She'd never imagined a man's body could be so attractive. Mark had been good looking in an easy sort of way. But Patrick... Corded muscles, smooth skin sprinkled with silky hair. Those angry scars on his shoulder meant something, for when she touched them she could feel his heat in her fingertips.

"So much for not thinking about him," she grumbled.

"What's that, lass?"

Shaking her head, she snapped the book closed.

"Nothing, Seamus." She came to her feet. "I believe I'll go to bed."

Seamus glanced at the clock and arched one red brow at her. He shrugged his slight shoulders. "Good night then,

Tara."

"Good night."

She went down the hall to her bedroom. She stripped down to one of her borrowed slips and unpinned her hair. Sitting at the pretty little vanity, she regarded her reflection. She'd changed since coming here. Her complexion was brighter and her hair silky. It must be the fresh air and that creamy soap she used in the shower. She thought for a second. Patrick had run his fingers through her hair there in the woods, making that sexy sound in the back of his throat.

"Enough!"

She turned her back on her reflection and crossed to the bed. Settling beneath the soft linens, she punched her pillow and squeezed her eyes shut.

***

Patrick prowled the woods, unable to sleep. It wasn't lust that drove him deep into the trees tonight. There was no witch waiting to lead him into sin here. Nay, 'twas Tara.

The memory of her. The lure of her. He wanted her. The tightness in his breeches was all the evidence he needed. But he wanted more than her delectable body and her sweet lips. He wanted her kind heart and her pure soul.

The lass loved Devlin. And his son loved her. The way Devlin said her name told Patrick as much. But she didn't belong here. He told himself that now for the hundredth time. But when he'd held her close, his body recognized what his mind fought even now. She was his!

He reached over his shoulder and touched his scars. The skin itched and tingled beneath his fingertips and he pulled away. Clenching his fist, he turned on his heels.

He wouldn't find relief here in the woods. The best he could hope for was another night of fitful sleep on his lonely pallet in the workshop.

***

"Pa.... Papa?"

Tara froze, turning in her seat to face Devlin. The boy looked right at her, his eyes clear.

"Papa?" he asked again, turning toward the front door.

She heard the footsteps Devlin had and knew Sean would soon walk into the house. And the little boy would be disappointed again.

"No, sweetheart," she said softly.

"Bloody fool," she heard Seamus mutter.

Devlin retreated a bit into himself, his little mouth

drawn in a line.

"Good evenin'," Sean boomed.

Tara smiled at the man, unable to keep from wishing he was someone else. Someone Devlin wanted so desperately to see. And she did too, but that was a thought best not considered right now.

Sean ruffled Devlin's hair, but the boy held himself still. Anger burned in Tara's belly, and from the scowl on Seamus's face she knew she wasn't alone. Why didn't anyone tell Patrick the truth? He was needed here. By his son, she quickly corrected.

Dinner was subdued despite the conversation kept up by Seamus and Sean. Tara found she couldn't summon more than polite answers. She kept her eyes on Devlin's slumped little shoulders, holding her own emotions in check.

When dinner ended, she saw Devlin to bed. He looked so lost, and there was a slight pout on his lips.

"You're sad, Devlin," she said for him. "It's all right. Tomorrow will be another lovely day and we'll play outside in the yard."

His eyes shifted toward the row of dolls perched on the table beside his bed. Tara reached for the Patrick doll, holding it out to Devlin. The boy gave a tiny shake of his head and she placed the toy back on the table.

"What story would you like to hear tonight, Devlin?" The boy offered nothing of encouragement, though she persevered. "How about the one with the little girl and the bears?"

She told him the story from memory, watching him for any sign of the enjoyment he usually took in her stories. But tonight he stayed quiet and immobile.

When she finished, she came to her feet.

"Good night, sweetheart," she said, her throat tight.

Devlin closed his eyes tight and she sighed. Rising to her feet, she squared her shoulders. Oh, she'd make sure the little boy wouldn't know tonight's rejection and hurt again.

She closed the door behind her when she left the room. If she had to go to Patrick and drag him home, she would.

***

Patrick returned to the shop, after another lonely walk did little to ease him. His body burned with passion. His mind churned with guilt. Lord, he was a miserable excuse for a man. He let himself into the shop and slammed the door shut.

"About time you got here."

He froze, narrowing his eyes to make out a slight female form standing in the middle of the shop.

"Tara?"

Was that a soft curse he heard her utter?

"Yes," she sighed.

He went to the lantern on his workbench and turned up the flame. When he turned he found her standing with her arms crossed, her brow furrowed.

"What the devil are you doing here?"

She clicked her tongue. "I could ask you the same thing."

"You walked here?" He glanced out at the dark night, finally arching a brow at her. "Alone?"

"It was still light out when I left," she countered. "After I put a very disappointed little boy to bed, I couldn't just let this go."

Patrick sat down on his pallet, keeping as far from Tara as he could.

To his surprise she stepped closer to him. "Don't you see what you're doing to Devlin, Patrick? Every night you say away?"

"He's getting better," he grumbled.

She nodded. "Yes, he is. But no thanks to you. He needs

you."

"Nay, lass. We've discussed this."

"No!" She let out a breath and held her hands at her sides. "You decided to take yourself away from your son. He's connected to you, Patrick."

Patrick rested his head in his hands. "Nay. It's not a natural connection."

"What do you mean? Oh, that." She waved one graceful hand through the air. "So you're a Braunach. So what?"

He looked up at her in surprise. "You know? Who told you?"

She shrugged and sat down beside him, her thigh brushing against his. He fought the urge to turn and pin her beneath him on the narrow bed, and focused intently on the toe of one of his boots.

"I knew there was something there," she said. "Devlin seemed... different. Otherworldly, sort of. And then Luke said something about MacDonald gold and it all made sense. Once Brianna explained it, that is."

"Luke and Brianna?" He thought of what his family said of Tara and their gold, of her value. He lifted his head to face her. "What else did Luke say?"

Even by the meager light he could see her pretty blush. "N-nothing, really. But that's not why I'm here."

He moved a fraction closer to her, taking some pleasure in the widening of her pretty amber eyes. She wasn't as unaffected as she pretended to be. Suddenly he had no desire to send her from him.

"Why are you here, lass?"

She licked her lips and he watched the motion, his breath coming fast.

"Tara," he began, his voice a warning he wished he could heed.

She leaned toward him, her lips parted. He could see her little pink tongue just inside her mouth and wanted to taste her again.

Suddenly she jerked away, jumping to her feet. "Oh no, you don't! You won't charm me again, Patrick MacDonald!"

He bit back a curse. She thought he was trying to charm her? Nay. He had seduction on his mind, damn his guilt.

"I wasn't tryin' to charm you, Tara."

She gestured toward the bed, her mouth moving. "Then what was this?"

He stood and gathered her in his arms.

"This, lass?" He kissed her, catching her sigh in his mouth. He brought his lips to her ear. "This is passion, Tara."

Chapter 14

Tara closed her eyes, letting Patrick's soft touch and lyrical voice wash over her. This wasn't right, her mind screamed. Oh yes, it was! her body countered. She leaned her head back, her eyes drifting closed.

"Patrick," she murmured.

Was that her voice, all husky and pleading?

"Aye, lass," he rasped.

He held her tightly, dropping kisses over her throat. She reached her arms around him, pulling him closer to her. When she ran her hands over his back, his shoulders, he wrenched out of her arms.

"Nay!" he roared.

She opened her eyes and stood there, her arms still reaching toward him. He pulled away as Devlin did, backing against his workbench to hang his head. Silent sobs shook his big body and she felt his despair as acutely as she did Devlin's.

"Patrick?"

"Ah, it's no use, Tara."

She felt cold seep into her, and her passion was a distant memory.

"I don't understand," she whispered.

He lifted his head to stare hard at her. He was so much like Devlin, she thought. Saying so much with those gorgeous blue eyes. She could read his hurt and pain and desire.

"I'll walk you home," he stated.

She glanced at the rumpled blankets on that cot and knew it was for the best. And if night hadn't come while she waited for him, she'd tear out of the workshop and run home alone.

"Yes." She ran a hand over her heated cheeks. "Thank you."

The walk back to Seamus's house began in silence. But with him beside her, her attention focused on putting one foot in front of the other, she could voice the concerns that had driven her to the workshop in the first place.

"You need to take an active part in Devlin's therapy, Patrick."

"Nay," he said, his voice firm.

"He needs the connection," she insisted. "He looks for you every night at dinner. Every morning when he wakes up."

Patrick was quiet. She chanced a look at him, finding

him frowning with uncertainty.

"But I only had him a few days before bringing you here, lass. He needs you more than me."

"I don't know why you stay away from him, Patrick. It's not my place to judge you."

He spat out a curse. "You're the only one, then."

She stopped and reached out to grab his arm. "Your family loves you." She released him and pressed a hand to her breast. "Look, I never had a real family. I'd give almost anything to have one like yours."

He stared into her eyes, his expression raw. She pulled back at the emotion there.

"You deserve a family, Tara." He began to walk again, his face shuttered. "I don't."

She couldn't say anything to that dark statement.

"Devlin deserves a family, too," she said.

"He's a MacDonald," he muttered. "He has the whole family."

"But he has no parent." She took a breath and asked the question that had been torturing her almost since he brought her here. "Who's Devlin's mother?"

Patrick flinched as if she struck him.

"Devlin's mother… She…" Rage twisted his face and he spit on the ground. "That witch doesn't signify."

Tara couldn't make her mouth form words. Had this woman hurt him so much he couldn't even speak her name? That little bit of hope she hadn't even known she harbored shriveled in the pit of her stomach. Patrick's heart belonged to the woman. The hatred clear on his face didn't matter.

She continued on beside him, nauseated by her foolish dreams of belonging here. The truth struck her then, cold and hard.

She didn't belong anywhere.

***

Patrick stood in the shadows again, watching Tara playing with his son. Devlin followed Tara with avid eyes, his mouth pursed in concentration as he followed the ball in her hands. She waved it about, finally tossing it in his direction. With a little yelp, Devlin caught it. Patrick was stunned. His son caught the ball! He was actually playing with Tara!

"Very good, sweetheart," Tara beamed, hugging Devlin.

To Patrick's amazement, the child didn't pull away

from her embrace. Lord, if only Patrick could be as free as his son in that moment. Tara placed a loud kiss on Devlin's cheek, earning another hug from the boy.

Tara released him and urged him backward. "Throw it again, Devlin!"

Devlin didn't hesitate, but threw the ball into Tara's waiting hands. With another whoop of encouragement, Tara hugged him to her breast.

"You like playing ball, don't you sweetheart?" she asked, her breath ruffling Devlin's curls. "You play very well."

The little boy smiled. The expression was fleeting but Patrick would bet his best boots that the boy smiled. His heart gave a lurch. Devlin seemed so bright and clear in that moment. Patrick knew he'd hold the memory of that little grin for the whole of his days.

He watched the girl who had wrought this miracle. His Tara. He admired her, 'twas true. She'd adapted so easily to this time and place so different from her own, although Brianna's modern conveniences had to go a long way. She roused loyalty in all the MacDonalds without even trying, too. And now she brought Devlin back into the light and gave him the hope of a real life. Patrick sucked in a breath as his mind recognized what his heart knew. He was in love with Tara!

Tara was good and sweet. And passionate, his mind whispered. She loved his son. And more than once she'd endured Patrick's clumsy attentions. His body remembered her more than enduring his advances. She'd welcomed him last night in the workshop. If honor, and the memory of his sin, hadn't intruded, she would truly be his now.

His shoulder gave a twinge. His damn scar. That reminder of his sin. And his punishment. At least Devlin would be free of the Banshee's legacy.

Tara asked about the boy's mother last night. He cringed to remember what he'd said in response. His reaction to such a reasonable request was overblown. He'd said more in that outburst than he'd meant to, 'twas true. He could only imagine what Tara thought now.

She knew they were Braunachs. And that didn't matter to her? He believed she was sincere. In all the time he'd known her she was never anything but. But what would she think if she knew Devlin's mother was a Banshee?

He set thoughts of the witch aside and watched the two for a little while longer as they played with the dolls he'd made. He noticed one doll sat untouched. The one representing him. Disappointment filled him. Devlin needed his father, Tara insisted. Devlin needed the connection. Could that be true?

He looked at that lonely doll, exiled there on the stone wall. He wouldn't think about it. He wouldn't see the obvious comparison between the doll and himself.

"Oh, Devlin!" Tara laughed. "You want me to dance with you?"

Patrick watched as Devlin moved the two dolls representing himself and Tara. With another laugh Tara grabbed Devlin up in her arms. The child made a sound, guttural but there nonetheless. He very nearly laughed.

Patrick watched as Tara twirled his son in widening circles, catching Devlin's smile and Tara's answering grin. He loved his son. Devlin was more than a consequence of his madness with the Banshee. He was a part of him. A part of his heart. Tears pricked his eyes and his throat felt tight. He loved Devlin, and Tara too. That didn't matter. Tara loved Devlin. That was clear. They had each other, at least until he had to take Tara back to her own time.

He longed to give in to the driving need to be with her, to share her passion and her life. He'd thrown away caution and honor to bed the Banshee. He wouldn't damage Tara's heart that way.

His gaze fell on the Patrick doll, motionless and alone. He tore himself away from the gardens and went back to the workshop.

***

Tara held Devlin tight, delighting in every happy little sound the boy made. He hugged her about her neck, his lips moving silently. She didn't know what he tried to say, but he spoke to her heart. With every look and motion he gave himself to her. And she would hold this feeling close forever.

She wouldn't think about Patrick inevitably taking her back to the future. She wouldn't think about leaving this dear little boy or this warm and vocal family. And Patrick? Oh, she'd never love another man like she did him.

"Oh, you wore me out!" she giggled, settling on the low wall.

Devlin smiled and plopped down beside her, his two dolls still held close.

"Tara… tired."

She blinked. "Yes, sweetheart. Tara's tired. But happy."

Devlin nodded. He looked off toward the side of the garden, as if searching for something.

"Papa."

Tara started and turned, finding nothing but shadows beneath the thick trees bracketing the yard. She faced the boy again, a smile on her face.

"Your papa is at the workshop, Devlin."

Devlin gave a tiny shake of his head. He reached for the Patrick doll, once more fisting his hand before touching it. She watched as he steeled himself. He had a strong spirit. Like his father.

"Do you want to see your papa?"

Devlin slanted her a look, the yearning clear in his eyes. But he said nothing, and didn't nod or shake his head in answer.

"Your papa will come to see you soon," she said. "I promise you."

Devlin let out a breath and kicked his feet, staring at his shoes as they moved back and forth. She suspected he thought of Patrick still, as he'd done with the shoes almost from the start.

"Your papa loves you, Devlin." Devlin made no answer. "I love you, too."

He looked up at her, his eyes intent. He pointed to the

Patrick doll.

"I don't understand, sweetheart."

He took the Tara doll held so lovingly in his arms and placed it beside the Patrick doll. She could only stare, speechless. The child knew. And telling him would ease her mind.

"I love your papa, Devlin," she whispered.

He nodded, a look of satisfaction on his face. She hugged him to her once more, fighting the tears that stung her eyes.

Chapter 15

"Hi, Tara!" Bryce chirped. "We're here to see Devlin."

Tara looked up to find Brianna and her son standing in the doorway. She glanced at Devlin to gauge his reaction to the little boy hopping up and down with excitement. His face showed curiosity and just a little bit of surprise, to her relief. His eyes were round and his mouth an O.

"Come in!" Tara smiled and came to her feet. "We were just playing with Devlin's blocks."

Bryce's face lit up. "Oh, blocks are brilliant!"

With that, Bryce sat himself down right beside Devlin, chattering away as he stacked the blocks in front of his cousin. Tara watched closely for any sign of distress on Devlin's part, but the child watched Bryce with open interest.

Satisfied, she faced Brianna. "Hello, Brianna."

"Seamus suggested this, Tara." Brianna stepped into the room, her hands spread. "I hope it's all right."

"It's a lovely idea." Tara watched the little boy so much a part of her heart and shrugged. "I admit I've been keeping Devlin to myself these past weeks."

"And keeping to yourself," Brianna gently pointed out.

Tara gave a nod. "I know. I'm sorry I haven't been by to

visit. I haven't even gone outside, except for the backyard."

Brianna took Tara's wrist and tugged her toward the large bed. "Sit," she said. She settled down beside her. "Tell me what happened."

Tara eyed the boys and saw they were busy—Bryce playing and talking while Devlin watched him with awed eyes—and took a breath.

"I asked Patrick about Devlin's mother," she whispered, leaning toward Brianna. She held up one hand at her friend's stunned expression. "I know I shouldn't have, but I had to know why he stays away." From her? From Devlin? She couldn't say exactly. But he was as distant as her little apartment in Indianapolis.

"Devlin's mother isn't the reason," Brianna said sharply. She looked worriedly at the boys, who seemed unaffected, then back at Tara. "She doesn't matter."

"That's what Patrick said." Tara thought for a moment. "Well, not quite in those words."

Brianna shook her head. "Patrick blames himself, Tara. For everything."

Tara nodded. "I know. But he's so important to Devlin's recovery. I know that as sure as I know anything I learned in grad school." Tara looked at the little boy she now loved as her own. "He asks for him, you know."

"No," Brianna whispered. "That's brilliant!"

Tara sniffled and gave a little smile. "I know it is. It's amazing, actually. But I can't tell him why his father's not here, Brianna." She shook her head. "It breaks my heart."

"Tara," Brianna whispered, her eyes round. "You love him."

Tara's cheeks heated and she fingered the coverlet, her head down. "I do love Devlin. I admit it."

Brianna clicked her tongue.

"I can see right through you, Tara Connor," she stated.

Tara looked at her friend, opening her mouth to protest. In the next moment she surrendered the battle. "Oh, all right. I never was a very good liar."

Brianna grinned. "Another point in your favor, then."

Tara smiled. "I don't know what to do about this, Brianna."

Brianna patted her hand. "You've let your instincts guide you this far, Tara."

"My instincts?"

Brianna laughed softly. "You're in the year 1814, Tara. In a lovely but backward dell in what I think is possibly the prettiest part of Ireland. And after bugging out at first, your instincts have carried you."

"Mind-boggling, but true."

"Your instincts and your knowledge have taken Devlin so far."

The two women looked at the boys for a moment.

"It's all I can do," Tara admitted.

The boys were a study in contrasts, but the differences weren't as sharp as they had been. Bryce was the sturdier of the two, but Tara was happy to note that Devlin wasn't the waif he'd been when she'd first come here. Mrs. O'Grady's good food and the MacDonalds's attention had indeed brought changes to the little boy. Well, from nearly all the MacDonalds.

Devlin eased closer to Bryce, who offered his cousin one of the blocks. Devlin took it, holding it still for a moment. Then he slowly brought it to the stout stack Bryce had built, setting it on top. Bryce clapped his hands and nodded. Tara saw it in that instant, a smile from Devlin for the boy beside him.

"You like playing with Bryce, Devlin," Tara said.

Devlin nodded, offering her the most beautiful smile. Tara's heart jumped in response to this little Braunach's charm. It was pure and golden, and as bright as his coppery curls. Her eyes pricked with happy tears.

"Oh, Tara," Brianna said, her voice thick.

"I know," Tara said, smiling through her tears. "Isn't he wonderful?"

Brianna gave a firm nod.

"Spoken like a mother," she said in a low voice.

In that moment Tara wished Devlin was hers. That he had grown inside of her. But some other woman had had that blessing. A woman Patrick still couldn't let go.

"No." She swiped away her silly tears and shrugged one shoulder. "I'm not his mother."

They sat in silence for a few minutes, just watching the boys interact.

Bryce grabbed up Devlin's dolls, excitement on his face. He fingered the green ribbon around the neck of one of the dolls. "Oh, this one's Uncle Seamus!"

Devlin gave a jerky nod. Bryce lined up the family of dolls in a row.

"This is Uncle Sean," Bryce said, pointing to the black-haired one. He touched the small, curly-haired one. "This is you, Devlin. And this one is Uncle Patrick."

Tara watched Devlin as Bryce freely touched the Patrick doll. His little hands were clenched in fists in his lap and his body was held stiffly. That yearning was in his eyes, and Tara knew Brianna saw it too.

"I'll blister his ears," Tara heard Brianna promise.

Tara guessed that wasn't good for Patrick, and probably just what he deserved. But personally, she'd rather kick his ass.

"Tara," Devlin said, lifting the woman doll in his hands.

Bryce touched it gingerly, as if he knew how important the doll was to Devlin. The boy was as sensitive as his Pixie mother.

"She's pretty," Bryce said. "Like Tara."

"Tara," Devlin said again. "Papa."

Bryce handed him the Patrick doll but Devlin pulled away, shaking his head. Bryce placed the doll on the floor and Devlin scooted toward it. Once again he placed the Tara doll beside it. He gave a nod of satisfaction.

"Oh!" Bryce said. He giggled. "Tara and Uncle Patrick!"

Brianna laughed. She crossed her arms and shot Tara a look of triumph.

"Never mind," Tara said without anger. She got down on the floor with the boys. "Now, what do you boys say to playing in the backyard? In the gardens, maybe?"

Bryce jumped to his feet and Devlin mimicked the motion, though a beat slower.

"Come, loves," Brianna said, taking Bryce's hand. "Miss Tara says Devlin is very good at playing ball. Will you show us, Devlin?"

Devlin glanced at Tara, then nodded to Brianna. Tara's heart filled with pride as he placed his hand in hers and began to tug her toward the door.

"All right, sweetheart," she laughed. "We're going, already!"

The four of them went out into the sunny gardens. Tara put her dark thoughts about Patrick out of her mind and indulged in a bit of fantasy as she and Brianna played with their two little boys like any pair of mothers in any time or place.

***

"Brianna says Tara's growing attached to the boy," Luke stated.

Patrick looked at his older brother, feigning only mild interest. "It's natural, I wager."

"She's like a mother to him," Luke went on.

If only that were so, Patrick silently prayed. "Aye."

Luke busied himself at his workbench, with nothing of real importance that Patrick could see. He braced himself for more of his brother's meddling.

"Bryce played with Devlin."

"Nay!" Patrick held himself still. "How was Devlin?"

Luke flashed him a grin. "Devlin took to him, Brianna says. The two played like brothers."

Patrick ran a hand over his face, rubbing his eyes as he sucked in a breath. "God bless the lass," he whispered.

Eager to know all of it, he straightened and faced his brother. "Tell me everything."

Luke arched a brow. "Seems to me you ought to ask the lass."

Patrick gave an impatient shake of his head. "Nay, Luke. Tara will just... She's... Ah, she asks things of me that I can't give her."

"Like the truth?"

Luke's words struck him straight in the belly.

"Let it go," Patrick grumbled.

Luke muttered something more, but Patrick wasn't

about to ask him to clarify it. He forced his attention on the pair of lady's slippers he'd fashioned for Tara. They were of a soft kid leather the rich color of her hair. Lord, he was going daft.

"'Mornin', lads!" Sean called as he entered the workshop.

"'Tis about time you joined us, brother," Luke teased.

Sean shrugged, his usual grin a bit brighter this morning.

Patrick narrowed his eyes on his younger brother. "What are you grinnin' about?"

Sean laughed lightly. "Ah, I was just with the lovely Tara." Sean held up one hand. "Now don't be gettin' angry, Patrick. I just sat outside in the gardens with her and the little lad."

Patrick again felt that stab of jealousy, unwarranted though he knew it was. It was his own choice that Sean could step into the space Patrick had left empty.

"Oh?" he asked.

Sean snorted and turned to Luke. "The lass is amazin', Luke. Do you know she got Devlin to smile? To really smile?"

"Aye," Luke returned. "Brianna told me as much."

"He's the picture of you, Patrick," Sean added. He winked in Luke's direction. "Save for the smile, o'course."

Luke chuckled. Patrick kept his thoughts to himself as the talk turned to other topics. Devlin smiled? He marveled. Ah, if only he could have seen a bright grin on his son's face!

Perhaps Tara had the right of it. He polished the supple shoe until he could nearly see his reflection. Perhaps he should come and spend time with the boy.

Fear nagged at him. Fear that his presence would set Devlin back on the path he'd been on when he found him. Withdrawn and sad. Wild and lonely. 'Twas Tara's goodness that wrought this miracle. Her love that brought a precious smile to his face.

"...all comin' for dinner, then," he heard Sean say.

"What's that?" Patrick asked.

"We're all dinin' at Uncle's this Sunday after church," Luke explained. "You remember church, don't you, Patrick?"

"Aye," he said without anger.

He hadn't attended mass but for holidays since the mad time of his sin four years ago. And each time he missed church, each and every Sunday, the guilt had gnawed at him. And now that he had Devlin he stayed away to cease the whispers and stares. H wouldn't expose his son to the slights against the innocent boy the heartless villagers would make.

He knew Tara didn't take Devin to church. He had that from Sean. He wasn't surprised. She'd never leave Devlin open to the vile wagging tongues of the dell. He'd have to ask her if she prayed with him. If she sang the hymns to him. With her lovely voice, it would be a treat to be sure and sweeter than a choir of angels.

He finished with the slippers and weighed them in his hands. Perfect. He longed to put them on Tara's dainty feet, and to see her face flushed with embarrassment and delight as she thanked him for his gift. He placed them firmly down on the bench and clenched his hands.

"Sean, you'll take these to Tara this evenin'?"

Sean and Luke exchanged a look of confusion.

His younger brother eyed the slippers and shrugged. "Aye. They be pretty shoes. I'm sure Tara will like them."

Patrick gave a nod, his lips pressed in a line. He turned his attention to the stout work boots the blacksmith ordered, seeing nothing but Tara's delight when she received his meager offering.

It was a small thing, but his heart felt a bit lighter.

***

Tara sat in the living room with Devlin perched on her lap.

221

She reasoned he should start spending some time in the rest of the household, and staying in the parlor with the family was an excellent start. As they looked at a picture book of animals, Tara named each one and urged Devlin to repeat after her.

"That's a cow, Devlin," she said.

Devlin screwed up his eyebrows. "C-cow."

She praised him and gave him a squeeze. She caught Seamus's eye where he sat cross-legged in his green chair. The man smiled at her, pleasure in his eyes. Pleasure and relief, which told her he loved his little great-nephew as much as Tara did. She turned her attention back to the book, her mind on Seamus.

Something about the man was familiar, though she'd not given it much thought over the past couple of weeks. Surely he didn't remind her of the father she'd never known. And none of her mother's loser boyfriends had the spark of affection she saw in Seamus's green eyes. Maybe her favorite advisor, the man who urged her more than once to take advantage of grants and scholarships she'd been afraid she hadn't earned.

"You have more talent than you think, lass," Seamus

said.

Tara started. That was something Dr. Everett had told her time and again. One look at Seamus and she read the twinkle in his eye. Could he know that his offhand comment would have such a reaction? Did the Braunach charm extend to mind reading? God, she was in trouble if that were true. Every day she felt more at home in this place and time than the faraway place she'd had in Indianapolis.

Dinner tonight had been a quiet one, perfect for a Monday after the fun and noisy affair of the previous afternoon. Yesterday all the MacDonalds had crowded into Seamus's dining room, fresh from church and looking fine. Mrs. O'Grady had been flush with pleasure to serve all the family. All but Patrick, of course. Tara hadn't taken Devlin to church, however. The venom the villagers reserved for the innocent little boy still turned her stomach and she wouldn't expose him to it.

But after church the two little boys had greeted each other like fast friends, Bryce with a loud hello and Devlin with a nod and smile. Despite the number of people at the table, no one sat in Patrick's chair. Luke had begun to, but Devlin's choked denial urged him to leave the seat vacant. Stupid man, that Patrick.

"Your cousin Bryce asked after you today, Devlin," Sean

said from his place opposite Tara. "He came to the workshop to visit his papa."

At the cherished word, Devlin's head shot up. Tara saw the regret on Sean's face.

"Ah… Those are pretty shoes, Tara."

Tara hid her smile at his awkward change of subject, but she held out one foot for Devlin to see.

"Your papa made these shoes, Devlin. Like he made yours. Aren't they pretty?"

Devlin reached down to run his fingers over the softest leather Tara had ever felt.

The little boy gave a nod. "Mac…"

"MacDonald shoes, Devlin." Sean grinned. "Aye, you're a sharp lad."

Devlin offered his uncle a smile. Sean seemed to fill the child's desire for his father, at least for this brief moment. Nothing more was said of Patrick, and Tara returned to their picture book. She glanced at Sean where he sat playing chess with Seamus. He was very handsome and strong. Back in Indy he'd have no problem picking up any woman he wanted, either on campus or in a downtown bar. He was easy going, too. The contrast between him and Patrick couldn't be stronger. Patrick was as dark as the night and Sean was as bright as the sun.

Later, after she tucked Devlin into bed, she headed back out to the living room. She stilled as she heard what sounded like an argument between Sean and his uncle, and turned toward her bedroom.

"'Tis a shame, it is," Sean grumbled.

"Don't be tellin' me," Seamus answered. "Bloody fool don't see what's before him."

"He cares for the lass, Uncle," she heard Sean say. "He can't deny it."

Tara froze. Seamus made a sound like a grunt.

"And why shouldn't he? Our Tara be the finest lass I've met. As much as Luke's Brianna."

"She loves the little lad," Sean said.

"Aye. And Devlin loves her."

A wistful sigh met her ears, though she couldn't guess from whom.

"'Tis a pity, to be sure," Seamus said.

"I think she loves the fool," Sean said simply.

Her heart began to pound. Oh, did everyone know what was in her heart? Did Patrick? Embarrassment filled her and she turned, hurrying to her room. Tears came quickly, but they were blessedly silent.

It didn't matter what she felt for Devlin's father. His heart and soul was held by Devlin's mother. And the affection the MacDonalds had for her wouldn't make a difference when she finished her work with Devlin.

She wiped at her eyes and stared at the plaster ceiling above her very pretty nineteenth-century bed. She wouldn't think about how comfortable the furnishings were or how well she fit into this life. Patrick wouldn't be swayed. Didn't he stay away from his son out of his feelings for the boy's mother?

She had spent most of her life in a place where she never truly fit in. She was damned if she'd spend the rest of it in a place where she never would!

Chapter 16

Tara swallowed her tears as she watched Devlin playing with his dolls. She planned to order Patrick to return her to Indianapolis, and soon. But she knew leaving his son would break her heart in two.

The late-morning sunlight streamed through the window behind Devlin, accentuating that quality she'd first sensed and now knew to be magic. He was a Braunach, she knew. And dearer to her than any child she'd know in the real world. Amazing.

"Tara," the little boy said, holding one doll close to him. "Tara... loves Devlin."

Oh God, how could she leave him?

"Yes, sweetheart," she smiled.

He placed an awkward kiss on the doll's little face and flashed his shy smile. My, he was a little charmer. That brought her up short. That MacDonald charm was the reason she was here, wasn't it?

She settled down beside him, running her fingers over the other dolls neatly arranged on the floor. The Devlin doll was flanked by Sean and Seamus's representations but the Patrick doll was off to one side, as usual. The child still watched the doll with longing, even scooting closer to it as they played quietly. Emboldened, she lifted the Patrick doll in her hands and held it in front of Devlin.

"Your papa loves you too, Devlin."

A mulish pout twisted his mouth.

"Nay," he said.

She blinked. Such clear emotion showed on his face, and she could read his anger and hurt.

"Devlin," she began, touching his shoulder. "Your papa does love you. He's just..."

What could she say? He loved the boy's mother so much he couldn't bear to look at her child?

Devlin grabbed the doll from her hand, scowling into the little stitched face. Tara held her breath.

"I...," Devlin croaked, his lower lip trembling. He clutched the doll to his chest, his eyes shut tightly. "I want Papa!"

"Oh, Devlin," she whispered. She wrapped her arms around him, rocking back and forth as he sobbed against her breast. "I know you want your papa. Shh. It's all right."

When he quieted, she lifted his chin in her hand. Tears spiked his long lashes and glistened on his cheeks. Real tears! She wiped at his cheeks and gave a nod.

"I'll bring your papa to you, sweetheart," she said. "I promise."

He sniffled and nodded in return, wrapping his arms around her neck. She'd keep her word to him. She would bring Patrick MacDonald back where he belonged if she had to drag his big body the whole way!

For the rest of the day, she thought of the best approach to bring Patrick home. She feared this would be the greatest challenge she'd ever faced. Her years of psychology and behavioral studies should've made it easy for her, but her heart wasn't engaged in her studies and cases in Indianapolis. She not only loved Devlin as her own. She loved Patrick, too.

After dinner that night, she tucked Devlin into bed.

"Good night, Devlin," she whispered.

He didn't return Tara's kiss good night, but trembled as he buried his head in the pillow.

"Papa," he murmured.

She grabbed the doll from its place on the bedside table and handed it to him, taking a breath as the little boy once more hugged it tight. That was it. She wouldn't let another day pass with Devlin so desperate for his father.

***

Patrick stretched out on his pallet. The sun was just setting, and he couldn't wait for sleep to bring him into the next day. The workshop was quiet, and the sound and chaos of the MacDonald house was something he never thought he'd miss. He wouldn't think about them now, laughing and talking as they sat around Uncle Seamus's drawing room. He knew Tara would be in the middle of it, so lovely and sweet. She'd truly wrought a miracle with Devlin. Soon it would be time to take her home, though. Damn him and his promise to her.

He ran his hands through his hair and sighed. He'd have to be a real father to Devlin after she'd gone. Would the boy want any part of him? Devlin's problems were solely his fault. How could he look into his son's eyes with anything but guilt?

And Tara…. Lord, how could he look at Tara again after his outburst.

"Patrick?"

He jerked his head toward the doorway, stunned to find Tara there again. He blinked and sat up.

"Tara."

She shrugged. "You left the door unlocked again."

He couldn't say anything as he ran his gaze over her. She wore her hair up, as had become her fashion since coming here. A lovely dress of pale yellow made her skin glow in the pink light streaking into the workshop. He saw she wore the slippers he'd made for her, and the gesture filled him with the same pride he'd felt as he watched Devlin play with the dolls. Well, with the dolls save one.

"You're here alone again."

She waved one hand. "Look, I came here for one reason, Patrick. To bring you to your son."

He came to his feet.

"Ah, lass. We discussed this."

She crossed her arms and tilted her head to one side.

"That was no discussion!" Her eyes flitted over him, warming his flesh. "You tried to charm me into agreeing with you."

He turned from her, suddenly realizing how he was dressed. He wore only his breeches. Hell, she'd seen the scar already, damn it! Turning, he faced her again.

"You shouldn't be here, Tara."

"Neither should you."

He sat down on the pallet. "Devlin doesn't need me, lass."

She stepped closer. "He needs you, you fool! He cried for you tonight, Patrick. Real tears!"

Patrick stared at her. "He cried?"

She sniffled, and he saw the tracks of tears on her cheeks.

"He wants you, Patrick. He needs you!"

Tara shook with emotion. He stood and wrapped his arms around her.

"You love the lad, Tara. Aye, you do."

She nodded against his chest, relaxing in his hold. Desire bit him hard, in his body and his heart. Ignoring his body's urgings, he sat on the pallet and pulled her down beside him. He held her for a few minutes, at last releasing her when she seemed to recover herself.

"Excuse me," she whispered, pulling out of his arms. "I shouldn't have."

He shook his head and watched her silently.

"I know how you feel about Devlin's mother, but—"

"What?" He gaped at her. "What's this about his mother?"

"You still love her."

"How the devil could you think that? Tara, lass. I never loved Devlin's mother."

"But you're still so angry at her."

He grabbed her by the shoulders. "Tara, Devlin's mother isn't…. She doesn't signify."

"You said that before, Patrick. But your feelings are so strong for her. You can't deny that."

Patrick snorted. "That witch doesn't deserve Devlin."

Tara stood, turning from him. "You see? Oh, it doesn't matter." She faced him again. "Look, marry her if you want to. I don't care. I'm here about Devlin and I won't let you distract me."

Patrick knew he couldn't keep the truth from her any longer.

"Ah, Tara. Let me tell you about Devlin's mother."

She rolled her eyes and held her hands in front of her. "Oh, I don't think so."

He grabbed her waving hands and stilled them. "Tara, you have to hear this. It'll at least make some kind of sense."

Tara, her face still showing her disbelief, sat down beside him once again.

"Tara, Devlin's mother is a Banshee."

233

***

Tara stared at Patrick, unable to speak. A Banshee? A wailing wind? A spirit?

"What the hell are you talking about?" she blurted out.

Patrick smiled without humor.

"A witch, lass. With a beautiful face and an ugly soul."

He didn't sound like a man smitten with Devlin's mother now.

"Okay, you're a Braunach. That I somehow believe. But a Banshee, is it?"

"Four years ago, lass. She… Well, she tricked me. Ah, I was a willing victim."

"You don't have to tell me this."

He grabbed her shoulders again. "But I do. I never loved the witch, Tara. 'Twas a sin, that lust. And I didn't know about Devlin until a few days before I jumped to Indianapolis."

Tara's head spun. Devlin's mother was a witch? An ugly soul, Patrick said.

"That darkness in him," she murmured. "That's what's been holding so tightly to his little soul."

Patrick nodded. "Aye, you have the right of it."

"But that doesn't explain why you refuse to see him. You love him, Patrick. I saw that the first night."

Patrick's brows rose. "Ah, you be a perceptive lass."

Tara flushed slightly at his praise. "Tell me, then. Tell me what happened."

Patrick stood, nodding his head as he began to pace.

"For weeks she lured me into the woods, Tara. I can't tell you how many times I told myself to ignore her call. But she caught me time and again." He spat out a curse she didn't recognize. "I knew it was a sin. I never told my family about the Banshee. Or about my dishonor."

Tara longed to ask him all of it, but held her tongue. Whatever passion he felt for the Banshee, he had no tender feelings for her.

He pointed to the scars on his shoulder. "She marked me, lass. As surely as placin' a brand on my flesh."

Tara studied the lines of ridged skin. They seemed fainter than that day in the woods, but it could be a trick of the light.

"I knew nothing of the child, Tara." He stopped pacing and faced her. "I swear to God I knew nothing of Devlin until the old witch sent for me."

"What old witch?"

"The Banshee's aunt. Aye, I know this be strange for you to understand, lass. We Faery folk take this all for granted, being born and raised here in the dell. But family ties, they're the same among the Faery as among the mortals."

She offered him a small smile.

"I've seen the love between Luke and Brianna, Patrick. And she's a Pixie."

Patrick returned her smile, though the expression was fleeting.

"Aye." His brow furrowed as he began the rest of his tale. "The old witch sent for me. She was dying and told me I had to take the child. Damn it, Tara. If you'd seen the way he lived with the old Banshee. Like an animal."

She reached out and touched him, drawing her hand back as he flinched. She gentled her touch, easing toward him as she would with Devlin.

"You gave him a home, Patrick. You gave him a family."

He eyed her. "You brought him back, lass. You made him part of the MacDonalds."

She stared at the floor. "And you have to give him a

father, Patrick."

He sank down onto the cot beside her. "Nay."

The word was rough, as if it came from a place deep inside him. She touched his hand where it lay on his thigh, gently grasping his fingers.

"He loves you, Patrick. Your family loves you."

"They know of my shame, Tara. And Devlin? Ah, I don't deserve any of them."

She longed to touch him, to lift his chin and make him look her in the face as she did with Devlin. But she was afraid he would just pull away. That darkness in his soul kept its lock on him.

"You are a MacDonald, Patrick. If I learned anything these past weeks, it's the importance of that distinction. You have your family's love. You're so very blessed."

He waved one hand.

"Nay. I'm not worthy of their love."

"Oh, you are a bloody fool!" she shouted.

"How can you say that to me?"

She jumped to her feet. "They love you! If I were lucky enough to belong to such a family, you couldn't tear me away from them!"

He stood, his blue eyes blazing. "Do you mean that, Tara?"

She nodded. "Yes. Don't you see what's right in front of you?"

He looked her over, slowly and thoroughly. Desire showed in his eyes before he shook his head.

"Aye, lass. If only I was worthy of you."

Chapter 17

Tara gasped as Patrick took her in his arms once more. All tenderness and passion now, he murmured sweet words in her ear as he ran his big hands over her back.

"Tara, lass. Do you think I'm worthy of your love?"

Tara couldn't deny it any longer, not while he held her so close.

"I love you, Patrick."

He pulled back, his blue eyes dark as he stared down at her.

"Ah, Tara."

At last he kissed her, and Tara wound her arms around his neck. She felt hot all over, as if every nerve ending urged her closer to him. He danced her backwards and she felt the cot at the back of her knees. The next moment he eased her down on the cot, kissing her ear, her throat.

"You're in my heart, lass," he said, his breath hot on her skin. He kissed her neck, flicking his tongue out to tease her flesh. "You're mine."

Tara couldn't answer, her pulse pounding in her ears as he kept up his gentle assault. He ran his hands over the front of her, and her thin dress allowed every touch to penetrate. He had such strong hands, as she'd always known. And such a tender touch she never could have imagined.

She stroked his back, feeling the muscles clenching as he pressed against her. When she reached the scar on his shoulder she tensed for his withdrawal, but he only kissed her harder.

His fingers fumbled with the tiny buttons on the front of her dress, soon easing the fabric away from her shoulders. The spring evening was cool and his mouth was hot as he kissed her breast, pulling on her nipple through the thin cotton slip.

"Patrick," she breathed, arching toward him.

"Aye, Tara," he rasped. "Aye."

He kissed and teased as her hands slid down his back to his butt, pulling him against her, closer still. His body was so hard. So demanding. She wanted to give herself to him, to have this moment forever etched on her when he brought her back to Indianapolis.

He lifted his head, urgently whispering her name. Tara opened her eyes to find him staring down at her. His gaze held her, sparkling with his MacDonald charm and something she didn't dare hope for. She touched his cheek and he closed his eyes and turned his head, placing a kiss on her palm. He faced her again.

"Lass?"

She knew what he asked. And she'd never wanted anything as much as she longed to give in to him.

"Yes, Patrick," she said softly.

***

Patrick sucked in a breath as he looked down at her, amazed at the desire lighting her amber eyes. When she had touched his scar, he'd felt no pain, just a screaming in his body for release. He told her she was his. Aye, he knew it. This girl, from another place and time, touched his heart. Tara brought him home.

"I love you, Tara."

She blinked up at him, her eyes clouded with cautious hope. He was a bloody fool to put that mistrust there.

He bent his head once more and kissed her, reaching down to lift her skirt. She lifted one leg, bending at the knee to draw his touch. Silently thanking the Lord for giving him this woman, he stroked the silken skin of her inner thigh. As he reached her drawers, he shook with desire. She was hot and soft and he was nearly lost.

Her fingers ran over his back again, easing around the front to trailed down his belly. She reached the buttons on his breeches, and Patrick leaned up on one elbow to allow her access. He sucked in a breath as her fingers brushed over his arousal. He grabbed her hand and brought it to his lips.

"Easy, lass." He softened his warning with a grin. "You're driving me wild."

She smiled up at him, seductive and wanton and apparently very pleased with herself. Aye, she was worth more than all the MacDonald gold. He was a lucky man.

Bringing his lips to hers, he kissed her again as he fumbled with his breeches. He prayed for control, but his self-imposed celibacy and Tara's delectable body and loving heart nearly caused him to disgrace himself.

One button undone.

Two buttons.

"Patrick!" Sean called from outside.

Patrick jerked as if shocked, certain he'd heard wrong.

"Patrick, what's going on?" Tara whispered.

Tara was as breathless as he, and he shook his head at her in response.

"It's nothing, Tara."

He brought his mouth to hers.

"Patrick!" Sean cried again, pounding on the door.

"Come quickly!"

Patrick cursed and came to his feet, refastening his breeches as he shot a warning glance at Tara. She looked up at him as he shrugged into his shirt, her hair tousled and her cheeks pink. Her dress was gathered around her waist, showing him her shapely legs and thin drawers. He'd kill his brother, he decided. He'd drag Sean's body through the dell and—

"Patrick, what be ailin' you?"

Sean rushed into the room, screeching to a halt as he took in the scene. Tara's eyes were wide with alarm, her mouth an O. Patrick stepped in front of the pallet, hopefully blocking the delectable Tara from his brother's prying eyes.

"What is it, Sean?" Patrick growled.

Sean gaped at Tara as she came to her feet, her dress now more or less in order. He quickly shook his head and wore a look of alarm on his face, an expression that sent Patrick's irritation fleeing.

"My God, man! What's the trouble?"

"The Banshee, Patrick. She came back."

Patrick's heart pounded low and deep as his stomach churned.

"Nay!" he rasped.

"Where's Devlin?" Tara asked.

Sean faced her, his eyes wild.

"She's got him, Tara. She be holdin' him. Demandin' to see Patrick!"

Tara went white. He thought for a moment that she would faint as she had in the woods when they leapt here, but then that strong spirit showed on her face and he knew just what she would do a moment too late. Before he could stop her, she ran past Sean and out into the night.

"Tara!" Patrick called.

He raced after her, his fear a white-hot thing in his belly. Fear for Tara and for Devlin.

Catching up to her, he grabbed onto her hand.

"Easy, lass," he panted.

Tara stopped and looked at him, her eyes shining.

"She has him, Patrick," she rushed out. "She has Devlin!"

Patrick gave her a jerky nod. "Aye. But she'll not have him. He's ours, Tara."

She began to protest, but Sean caught up to them before she could voice the doubt he saw in her eyes. They ran through the dell, bound for the house.

244

Before they arrived, the sound struck them. Whistling wind and a high wailing that sent a chill through Patrick's soul. 'Twas the Banshee's call. And far different than the one she'd use to lure him to his sin four years ago.

Patrick urged Tara behind him as they entered the house. The witch was holding fast to Devlin. Patrick stopped as he saw his son. Devlin was pale and slack, and all animation was gone from his little face and slight body beneath the Banshee's grip.

Patrick spied his uncle and Mrs. O'Grady among the furniture and books strewn about the drawing room, their eyes wild with terror. He motioned for Sean to join them, and turned his gaze to the Banshee again.

She was a beautiful as she had been those years ago, her thick golden hair wafting in an unseen breeze as she floated a few inches above the littered floor. Her dark violet eyes flashed as she flicked her gaze around the room.

"Keep away, you bloody Braunachs!" the Banshee screeched. She shook Devlin's body like it was one of his dolls. "Keep away or I'll kill the boy!"

"No!" Tara cried, rushing past him and into the house.

Patrick tried to grab on to her as she ran toward the Banshee.

245

"Tara!"

The Banshee turned toward Tara, waving her free hand to stop Tara's progress. Tara hit an invisible wall the witch had apparently built around her and Devlin, recoiling as shock registered on her face.

"Ya' can't be thinkin' to touch him, mortal!" the Banshee laughed. "Ya' ain't done enough to heal his sickness, have ya'?"

Tara squared her shoulders and took a careful step toward the witch. Patrick watched as her face showed the professional caring he'd seen in the Children's Hospital in Indianapolis.

"You're right," she said. "Devlin isn't the boy I hoped for. His recovery has been poor." Tara took a breath and let it out slowly. "He's sick and worthless and not fit to be a MacDonald."

"Lass, no!" Seamus cried.

Patrick knew in his heart what Tara was doing. She was smart and as cunning as a MacDonald. He caught Seamus's eye and the older man gave a tiny nod of understanding. Now Patrick could only pray Tara's intelligence was a match for the Banshee's dark magic.

"Ya' failed him, mortal," the witch hissed. "I left him to yer care and ya' did nothin' for him!"

Tara shrugged, the gesture seemingly casual. Patrick saw the trembling of her hands a second before she clasped them in front of herself. Again that professional mantle settled on her.

"I tried, I admit." She looked at Devlin and Patrick saw the love she felt for his son, and the fear she had for his safety. "He's a pretty thing," Tara went on. "But his soul is damaged."

Patrick saw Sean open his mouth to protest, but Patrick waved a hand to silence him. Hoping that Devlin was in no condition to hear the false, hurtful words, Patrick added his own to Tara's trick.

"It's true, witch!" Patrick said. "We don't want Devlin here in the dell."

The Banshee narrows her eyes on Patrick. "'Twas yer doin', MacDonald. Ya' ain't the pure soul I believed all those years ago."

It was Patrick's turn to shrug.

"It's your fault, witch. You seduced me, didn't you?"

The Banshee laughed, the sound both musical and frightening.

"Aye, Braunach. I seduced ya'. Was passin' easy, too."

"It's your fault, then," Tara put in. "It's your fault Devlin is the way he is now."

"Nay!" the witch cried. "I wanted a MacDonald to sire me babe, 'tis true. To cleanse me family lines."

Keeping an eye on Devlin, Patrick eased closer. He fixed a glare on the Banshee.

"You planned this, then?" Patrick asked.

"Aye!" the witch laughed. "I lured yer willin' body into the woods, MacDonald! Time and again." She flicked her head at Tara. "Did you tell yer little mortal whore how ya' came to me? Beggin' for it after but a couple o' times?"

Guilt slashed through him at the truth of the Banshee's words. He had gone to her, willingly seeking the sick pleasure she gave him as she took something else entirely from him. He didn't dare look at Tara, damning himself for a coward.

"You had your baby, didn't you?" Tara asked. "That's what you wanted."

The Banshee's lips curled in a sneer. "Aye. And when he was born I saw he had it still, the weakness of mind that doomed so many in me family."

"You left him with your kin, then?" Patrick asked.

248

"You abandoned your son?"

The Banshee waved one slender white hand. Patrick stared at it, still stunned that such beauty could hide such wickedness.

"The daft old witch took 'im," the Banshee said.

"You abandoned him," Tara stated firmly.

Devlin's mother glared at Tara and it was all Patrick could do to hold himself in check.

"Don't be sayin' that to me, mortal!" the witch cried. "He be sick, and yer magic was supposed to heal him."

Tara gasped.

"You sent Patrick to find me?"

The Banshee laughed.

"Nay! I didn't know the Braunach found somebody to help the boy 'til I learned the old witch died."

"Why now, then?" Tara asked. "Why have you come for Devlin now?"

"I been watchin' ya', mortal. I saw how the boy was." The Banshee shrugged. "'Twas time for me to claim 'im."

Patrick steeled himself for the lie.

"Take him, then," he said.

Chapter 18

Tara eyed Patrick with shock, but one glance from
those crystal blue eyes told her he was playing the Banshee
as Tara had been. The witch appeared to be all impulse and
emotion, and there would be no true reasoning with her.
She'd seen children locked in an endless loop of highs and
lows, but nothing in her studies or her work could have
prepared her for this encounter. Still, for Devlin—and for
Patrick—she would make certain that they put this bitch out
of their misery before she could do any more harm to her
family.

And they were her family. The MacDonalds were
everything she'd ever wanted and this was her home.
Standing strong and sending Patrick her strength in the only
way she really could, she caught his eye for a brief second.
She saw it. He was just as determined to grab their son from
the Banshee.

"You believe I would take him like this, Braunach?"
She shook Devlin again and Tara held back her protest even
as her heart leapt to her throat. "Yer son be damaged now."

Tara wanted to pull the fine golden hair from the
witch's head. She held Tara's dear boy in her tight grip, and

all light was gone from Devlin's eyes as he stared blankly back at her. He was as lifeless as the dolls they'd often played with, and she could hardly stand it.

"You take him, Banshee," Patrick said, putting a dose of glimmer into his words. Tara could feel it. That magic of his. "You wanted the child so badly."

"Not like this!" the witch cried.

"Take him," he said again. "He'll never be a true MacDonald."

The Banshee gaped at him, opening her mouth to let out a scream that broke the windows in the house. Tara covered her ears, forcing herself to keep her eyes on the confrontation between Patrick and his dark lover.

A howling wind began, and the books and papers on the floor circled the drawing room. Patrick visibly ignored the threat and crossed his arms, fixing a look of disinterest on his face as he braced his feet apart.

"Your screams don't move me now, Banshee."

The witch changed her tack in a flash, turning her seductive wiles in his direction. Tara felt the heat radiating from her supple form. In this instant, she was beautiful and compelling and all things sensual. Tara would be jealous of the Banshee's talents if she didn't know just how vile the creature truly was.

"Ya' wanted me, Patrick MacDonald." She ran a hand over her own curves. "Time and again ya' came to the woods, hard in yer breeches for me."

Tara fought hard to ignore the image of her Patrick going to the beautiful witch again and again. She knew he was a passionate man. Hadn't she been oh so willing to surrender to that passion barely an hour ago?

"You won't move me now, witch." Patrick's voice was firm. Cold.

Incredibly, the Banshee smiled, a radiance coming from her odd purple/black eyes. Even Tara felt her sensual pull in her chest, it was so palpable.

"Ya' want me still, MacDonald," the woman purred. "This pale mortal ain't be the one to ride ya' to yer pleasure."

Tara exchanged a look of worry with Sean, but Patrick's brother could only stare at the witch. His eyes were unfocused and his body held rigid. He must feel the pull of the Banshee, too. There would be no help there. Her eyes fell on Devlin then, still so limp in the witch's grasp. Anger boiled within her, anger that the Banshee would use her own son to exact revenge on her former lover. She wouldn't use Tara's beloved boy this way.

"Aye, witch," Patrick said, his voice so smooth now it struck Tara as a living thing. "You were incredible there in the woods."

The Banshee blinked, visibly affected by the full force of Patrick's charm. Tara knew then that he was only using his power to snare the witch. She would take the opportunity it gave her.

She crept closer to the child's slack hand, praying Patrick's potent charm would hold the woman's attention long enough. It seemed whatever barrier the witch had erected was gone for the moment.

"Come to me, Banshee," Patrick urged, his eyes sparkling.

"N-nay...," the witch faltered. She shook her head, her blond hair swaying. "Nay, MacDonald."

Patrick grinned, that same dazzling smile Tara couldn't ignore. The Banshee gave a jerk and Tara leapt toward Devlin.

She grabbed on to his hand and his eyes focused on her.

"Tara," Devlin said, his voice very small.

Tara pulled hard and wrenched the boy from his mother's grip.

253

"Nay!" the Banshee screamed.

"Over here, lass!" Seamus called.

Tara tugged Devlin along with her as she scrambled into the waiting arms of Seamus, who shielded them both from the Banshee. Devlin buried his face in her neck, sobbing as she rocked him.

"It's all right, Devlin," she whispered, feeling the burn of his tears against her neck. "I've got you now."

The witch howled and spun on Patrick. "Ya' charmed me, Patrick MacDonald!"

Patrick's beguiling grin was gone as he faced his former lover. "Aye, witch."

She screamed again. "Ya' tricked me! You and yer mortal." She shot a look of hatred in Tara and Devlin's direction, and Tara held the child closer still. The Banshee faced Patrick. "Ya' be havin' yer son now, Braunach."

Patrick gave a nod. "It's as I want it, Banshee."

The witch blinked in confusion. "What?"

Patrick smiled at Tara, and it wasn't anything like the false expression he'd used on the witch. No. This was a true smile that filled her with his love. Then he turned and faced the witch again.

"I love my son, witch," he said simply. "Despite his mother, I love Devlin."

Her shock was palpable. "Ya' can't be meanin' that, Patrick MacDonald!"

"I do," Patrick went on. "I promised the boy I'd help him. I made a promise to myself and to Devlin to see that he has the chance at a real life."

The Banshee's full, lush mouth turned down in a pout. "I seen how he is now. Better."

"Tara healed him. Aye, I brought her here against her will, but she healed Devlin's soul. She's the mother Devlin deserves."

Her rosy mouth twisted. "Ya' be in love with the mortal!"

Patrick gave a firm nod. "Aye."

The witch turned her shocked gaze at Tara, who came to her feet. Tara placed her arm around Devlin's shoulders as the boy faced his mother. She could feel a power in the little boy's frame as heat shot up her arm. It was strong and bright and truly magical.

"The little lad…," the witch began, her wavering voice giving away her confusion.

Devlin stared at the Banshee, his eyes clear and his stance strong. He raised his right hand, pointing one finger at the witch.

"Go," he said, his sweet child's voice strong and clear.

Patrick spared a glance at his son, a smile breaking through for an instant before he scowled at the Banshee.

"You heard the boy, witch," he said. "You can't deny his power."

The witch's shoulders slumped, and with that the wind died down as swiftly as it had started. The sucking sound of it stole Tara's breath.

"Aye, Braunach," the Banshee conceded. "The lad's power's as strong and pure as yer bloody honor." She faced Tara, hatred mixed with the resignation on her lovely face. "Ya' can have the little devil, mortal. He'll make ya' miserable the whole of yer days." She slid her gaze to Patrick. "And so will Patrick MacDonald."

With that, the Banshee flew out the front door of the house.

***

Patrick knew she wouldn't be back. Not for him and not for Devlin. She was forced to acknowledge the truth in Devlin's command, and even her parting shot at Tara was more smoke than fire.

"My God, lass," Patrick said, rushing to Tara's side.

"When you came up against the witch I nearly died."

Tara smiled up at Patrick. "He's all right, Patrick. Look at him."

Patrick looked down at Devlin to find the boy staring clear-eyed up at him.

"Papa," he said.

Patrick fell to his knees, grabbing the boy by his shoulders. "Ah, son. Pray, don't believe a word of what I told the witch when she had you." His throat was tight with tears as he gave the child a gentle shake. "You're good, Devlin. You're loved. You're a MacDonald."

Devlin smiled, and it was a sight more beautiful than Patrick had ever seen. The boy laughed then, and the sound was as light and pure as MacDonald gold. Patrick's heart soared as he saw this first true emotion from his son.

"I love you, Devlin," Patrick said, hugging the boy tight.

Devlin cuddled against his chest. "I love you, Papa!"

He cried then, holding on to Devlin. "I'll be the father you deserve, son. You have my promise on that."

Patrick heard Tara's sniffling beside him and closed his eyes. He silently thanked God for giving him this chance, this miracle. This redemption.

His family joined them then, loud and wonderful as they welcomed both Devlin and Patrick back into the MacDonald clan.

"Ah, laddie," Seamus beamed. "You came back to us, you did!"

Devlin grinned up at his great-uncle. "Aye," he giggled.

Sean ruffled Devlin's red-gold curls and the boy laughed again. Mrs. O'Grady mopped at her eyes with her apron, bending low to gently touch the boy's cheek.

"I'll fix ya' some of my biscuits, Devlin," she said with a nod. "Aye, that I will."

Patrick looked at his family, seeing the forgiveness that had always been there. Tara saw it, he knew. Tara had told him they would always love him. Ah, he'd been a bloody fool.

He released Devlin and stood, looking from Sean to his uncle. "Uncle, I don't know what to say."

Seamus waved a hand at him. "Off with you now, lad. 'Tis late and the little lad be needin' his sleep, I wager."

***

Tara stood off to one side as Patrick reconciled with his family and with himself. Devlin was whole and well. And she wouldn't wish it any other way.

"Come, son," Patrick said, lifting Devlin into his arms.

The child hugged his father as Tara watched. Patrick stopped as he turned down the hallway, glancing at her over his shoulder.

"Lass?"

Tara didn't wait for another invitation. She followed him to the bedroom, catching Devlin's twinkling gaze. He held her in his charm too, she thought with a smile.

"There you go, son," Patrick said, setting him on the little bed.

Devlin yawned as Patrick removed his shoes.

"Good night, Papa," he said softly. "Good night, Tara."

"Oh, good night, sweetheart," she said, bending to kiss his cheek.

Devlin smiled sleepily up at both of them before turning on his side. Tara sat beside Patrick. As she watched, the little boy settled himself for sleep, and his every motion was smooth and easy. Patrick was as quiet as she was, just drinking in the sight of Devlin falling gently into slumber for the first time in his life.

"I felt nothing for the Banshee, lass," Patrick whispered at last. "You know that, don't you?"

Tara hadn't known for sure, and she couldn't help but smile her relief.

"I'm glad to hear it," she admitted.

He turned toward her then, his brow furrowed. "He's well now, Tara," he said. "I can take you home if you wish it."

Tara shook her head. That connection, that belonging she'd unknowingly wished for her whole life, struck her straight in her soul.

"Patrick," she began. "I am home."

He smiled, the expression pure and bright. "Ah, lass."

He hugged her, and she returned the embrace. As she ran her hands over his back, she felt something different. Beneath her fingers, through his shirt, she could feel that his shoulder was smooth.

She pulled back and stared up at him. "Patrick, your scar."

"What?" He pulled at his shirt, baring his shoulder to her. "What is it?"

She touched his skin, which was smooth and clear beneath her fingertips.

"It's gone, Patrick," she said. "Your scar is gone."

Patrick reached over to feel it for himself. "The Banshee's mark," he rasped. He grabbed Tara to him again. "You healed me, lass. As well as you did Devlin."

Tara sighed as she settled against his chest.

"I'll be the man you deserve, Tara," he said. "You have my promise."

"You already are."

Epilogue

The day was crisp, and the sunlight beamed through trees ablaze with oranges and reds and yellows. The air was pure, and Patrick sucked in a breath as he stood on the steps of the church in the dell. He was marrying Tara this day, as incredible as that should be.

"Papa," Devlin said beside him, giving a tug on Patrick's black breeches.

Patrick smiled down at his son. "Aye, son?"

"Tara's my mama now?"

More than once both he and Tara had assured Devlin of his place in the MacDonald clan, and of the love they all had for him. They didn't know how much of his encounter with the Banshee the boy remembered, but there were still some nights when Devlin woke from nightmares and asked for him. And for Tara.

"Aye, Devlin. Tara will be your mama from now on."

Devlin gave a firm nod and turned to face the people now walking up the lane toward the church.

"Congratulations, Patrick MacDonald," the butcher said, a grin on his face. "Yer bride be a fine lass."

Patrick took the compliment, one of many he'd received

over the past weeks. The people in the dell had warmed to Tara's goodness. He smiled to himself. How could they not?

"Good morning," nodded the dressmaker. She ruffled Devlin's curls before dropping a wink in Patrick's direction. "Oh, the dress I made for you bride! She'll take your breath away, I daresay."

"I don't doubt that, Mrs. McKay," he returned with a bow of his head.

The lady laughed. "I best be joinin' her, then!"

The dressmaker entered the church, bound for the little room where his bride awaited the ceremony—hopefully with less impatience than he felt at the moment.

Patrick shifted in his shining MacDonald boots as he greeted more folks from the dell. Even the two blond lasses who had shunned both Tara and his son came to the ceremony, though their identical smiles seemed forced. Patrick couldn't have cared less. He was marrying his Tara and that was all that mattered.

He'd taken her back to Indianapolis after Devlin's startling recovery, still unsure if she'd wish to stay there. But she'd insisted her place was with him and Devlin, among the MacDonald family. Only when she'd arranged her affairs and begged him to take her home did he believe she really was his, body and soul.

Thank the Lord for Brianna. She brought Tara back and forth to the future on shopping expeditions, sparing Patrick the trouble if not the expense. He admitted he favored Tara's round little bottom in the future breeches she wore now and again, and the sneakers Devlin wore most days weren't bad, either.

Devlin tugged on his pants again. "There, Papa!"

Patrick looked down the lane as his family made their way toward the church. Seamus wore his usual bright green, and looked more dapper than ever in deference to the occasion. Sean was subdued in contrast, in both dress and demeanor. But Patrick's younger brother smiled as they approached.

"Beautiful day for a wedding, lad," Seamus beamed. He shook Devlin's little hand. "And don't you look the image of your papa, Devlin! Your mama will be so proud."

"Tara's my mama now, Uncle," Devlin said proudly.

"Aye, Devlin," Sean said. "You be a lucky lad there."

Luke and Brianna came next, urging Bryce between them. The two youngest MacDonalds greeted each other with hugs and giggles, at last pulled apart by Brianna.

"There now, boys. Can't have you less than handsome for this wedding."

Patrick shot her a look of thanks he hoped conveyed all he felt for Luke's wife. The woman was a friend and sister to Tara, and eased her way here.

"Brother," Luke grinned, nudging him with his shoulder. He looked at Brianna, now taking Bryce into the church, and leaned toward him. "I take it you be itchin' to get this over with, aye?"

Patrick rolled his eyes. His blasted honor demanded he keep himself from Tara's bed these past months, and the torture was greater than he'd imagined.

"Aye," he said, a wealth of meaning in the word.

Luke nodded. "See you inside, then."

The last of the guests arrived and Patrick and Devlin entered the church. Brianna had done a splendid job with the decorations, though he barely noticed the flowers dressing each trim pew. Tara's two men approached the altar, standing side by side as they waited for Tara to make her appearance.

When Uncle Seamus rose from his seat and hurried toward the back of the church, Patrick's heart began to pound. After what seemed like forever, his uncle escorted Tara toward the altar.

Ah, she took his breath away. Her thick sable hair was swept up and decorated with tiny white flowers to match her satin dress. Mrs. McKay hadn't been exaggerating. But he'd take Tara in clothing as simple as her future breeches and be grateful for her.

"Hello, Patrick," she said, her eyes bright and her cheeks pink.

"Hello, lass," he returned.

Seamus let out a sound of amused satisfaction and joined Sean and the family in the front pew. The priest, a round man who'd served the people of the dell for as long as Patrick remembered, smiled at the couple. And after but a few words, Patrick and Tara were joined together. Forever.

Patrick kissed his wife. When he lifted his head, Devlin eased his way between them.

"Mama!" he cried.

Tara bent to kiss him. Patrick lifted Devlin in his arms and the three of them smiled toward the congregation. They would raise Devlin together now, their child blessed rather than cursed with magic. Patrick had kept his promise to his son and to himself. His sin was absolved by love, and he knew his vow brought more than his son to him. It brought

Tara into his life, and he would keep his promise to her forever.

Author's note:

The Child with Special Needs

Stanley I. Greenspan, M. D., Serena Wieder, Ph. D.,
with Robin Simons

ISBN 020140764

About the Author

JoMarie DeGioia is a bestselling author of Historical and Contemporary Romance. She's known Mickey Mouse from the "inside," has been a copyeditor for her tiny town's newspaper, and a bookseller. A hybrid author, she also writes Young Adult Fantasy/Adventure stories, New Adult Romance and Paranormal Romance. She gets lost in DIY projects around the house and works out plot ideas during long runs. She divides her time between Central Florida and New England.

Discover books by JoMarie DeGioia

The Gentlemen Undercover series, including

A Hero and a Gentleman

The Dashing Nobles series, including

More Than Passion

Pride and Fire

Just Perfect

More Than Charming

The Cypress Corners series, including

Finding Harmony

Taming Jake

Loving Cassie

Winning Ben

The Gifted YA Fantasy/Adventure Trilogy,
including Gifted

The Baunachs of the Dell Series, including
Luke's Gold

Patrick's Promise

Connect with me online

Twitter: https://twitter.com/JoMarieDeGioia

Facebook:
https://www.facebook.com/JoMarie.DeGioia.Author

Website: www.jomariedegioia.com

www.ingramcontent.com/pod-product-compliance
Lightning Source LLC
Chambersburg PA
CBHW071455170626
46811CB00007B/2583